MARFA
SHADOWS

bright sky press
HOUSTON, TEXAS

2365 Rice Boulevard, Suite 202,
Houston, Texas 77005

10   9   8   7   6   5   4   3   2   1

DeMers, John, 1952-
Marfa shadows : a Chef Brett mystery / by John DeMers.
p. cm.
ISBN 978-1-933979-81-6 (hardcover)
1. Restaurateurs—Fiction. 2. Missing persons—Fiction. 3. Kidnapping—Fiction.
4. Indians of North America—Fiction. 5. Mexican-American Border Region—Fiction.
6. Organized crime—Fiction. I. Title.

PS3604.E4615M37 2010
813'.6—dc22   2009051366

Cover design and illustration by Mike Guillory
Printed in China through Asia Pacific Offset

MARFA SHADOWS

A CHEF BRETT MYSTERY

JOHN DEMERS

bright sky press
HOUSTON, TEXAS

This book is for my family, who no doubt wondered if I'd ever publish a book that was the type of fiction I read instead of the type of non-fiction I wrote. At Bright Sky Press, gratitude goes to editorial director Lucy Herring Chambers, who suggested I do this, as well as to Ellen Cregan and Rue Judd for their guidance and enthusiasm. Copy editor Victoria Ludwin kept me honest, as well as punctuated. For insight on the high-octane restaurant world this novel and its planned siblings describe, thanks to the chefs I've worked beside on cookbooks and other projects: Andrea Apuzzo, Andrew Jaeger and Dominique Macquet in New Orleans, Jimmy Bannos in Chicago, and Damian Mandola, Johnny Carrabba, Joe Mannke, David Denis, Aldo el Sharif and Carlo Molinaro in Houston.

That shadow, my likeness, that goes to and fro,
seeking a livelihood, chattering, chaffering;
How often I find myself standing and looking at it where it flits;
How often I question and doubt whether that is really me.

—WALT WHITMAN

MERIDYTH MORGAN WALKED INTO my restaurant, led by her bodyguard and followed by her driver. Yes, *that* Meridyth Morgan.

One of the men was short and wide, the other tall and wide. Both were deeply tanned, both wore dark glasses at night, and both had that taut, knotted thing going wherever their clothes had nothing better to do. They were like a fitness-center fantasy of Laurel and Hardy.

"Ms. Morgan," said the driver in Stetson and boots, with bangles and bows added to his suit in between, a cowboy as only somebody from Bayonne, New Jersey, can truly be a cowboy, "would like a table someplace private."

"You know," added the bodyguard, "someplace where she won't be bothered."

"Thanks," I smiled. "I've often wondered what the words 'someplace private' might mean."

Sometimes in this life, even for me, being a smartass isn't enough. It might play in Peoria, might impress a few hangers-on, or maybe bedazzle your own self-esteem for a moment or two. But deep down, in those times, no matter how old we are or cynical we pretend to be, we know we are shocked, we are shaken. We are seeing something, or in a few cases seeing *someone,* we never expected to see. And we shiver in that tiny hidden place where our lives are truly lived, because we know it was the thing we wanted most all along.

Turning quickly to hide how rattled I was, I led Meridyth and Co. to a four-top in a tiny side room, out of the restaurant's often-frenzied traffic flow. I smiled helpfully. She smiled but said nothing, even though I'm told all her movies are talkies.

I hadn't seen any of them, but then again, I own a restaurant and don't get out much. Her driver and her bodyguard didn't smile at all.

"This okay?" I asked.

"Yeah, bub, it'll do," the bodyguard said, not looking up as he pulled out the chair facing outward from the corner and let Meridyth slip into it.

By my reckoning, which has every reason in the world to be accurate, the second to last time I'd laid eyes on Meridyth Morgan in the flesh was when I was 17 and she was 14. Of course, I had lots of other things on my mind at the time—primarily the way my parents were busy turning an argument into a brawl into a divorce, one that would suddenly move me to Houston during Christmas break.

It was also the fourth quarter of the razor-close final game of my junior year—a game we won, by the way, beating a street gang of over-age roughnecks from up around Midland—under the lights of a stadium that isn't there anymore for a high school that no longer exists.

I caught a glimpse of Meridyth that second-to-last night through the space between my helmet and my facemask. And if her telling now is to be trusted, she caught a glimpse of me between her helmet of the strawberry blonde variety and the shimmer of her blue-and-gold pompoms. I can't really say it's Meridyth's fault, but I've always had a weakness for helmets of the strawberry blonde variety. Just ask my ex-wife, who's a brunette.

Laying eyes on her again, in my restaurant, wasn't the guessing game it so often is with people from your high school days. Meridyth's face—sometimes called "chiseled," but only if a chisel can wear kid gloves for taking the corners—her hair (still strawberry blonde, more or less) and her equally perfected biography had been pasted across any magazine our corporate Houston office got that wasn't about credit-card machines or industrial cleansers.

As a chef and a business owner, I ignored such gossipy rags, rejecting whatever passed for culture in America today. But even as my own life and marriage spiraled into the Texas-size mess that finally brought me home to Marfa, I followed in the broadest strokes the saga that made Meridyth Morgan a movie star and then, with her fame and money intact but her marriage to a young Italian director in shreds, brought her home too.

A little compare-and-contrast seems in order here, though. I returned to an abandoned café that became mine, more or less, when one of my father's longtime Mexican mistresses passed away. For sleeping quarters, I rent a one-bedroom adobe with a tin roof on the edge of town near Alamito Creek. It's no better than an apartment that's scared off all the neighbors. Meridyth Morgan bought, according to the tabloids, a 7,800-acre former cattle ranch from a dot-com zillionaire who went to prison in the border drug trade, a clever entrepreneurial venture that counted himself as its single most regular customer.

By this time, she was renovating the main house to resemble others of its ilk in Aspen, Telluride and St. George, and she'd announced plans via the weekly *Big Bend Sentinel* to host a film festival in the summer and turn most of her open land into a movie location. Perfect for those awkward moments, presumably, when she wasn't filming in LA or Venice or Beijing.

For a price, others would be welcome to make movie magic there as well.

My restaurant is called Mesquite, and if you read glossy food magazines of the sort I avoid at all cost, you've probably heard of us. I took the name, naturally, from the hard, hot-burning wood preferred for grilling and even for smoking here in West Texas, though every other part of the Lone Star State insists you have to use oak, hickory or pecan. And your grandfather's mesquite barbecue is a decent-size part of what we do here—at anything *but* your grandfather's prices.

As a fine-dining establishment, we serve the stuff with a variety of unexpected, Asian-tinged rubs and sauces, along with elevated Texas comfort food like chicken fried Kobe steak and sides that invariably hobble in on expensive crutches like lobster and truffle. We've been open for 18 months. And in the favorite phrase of a chef I long ago peeled shrimp and shucked oysters with in the French Quarter of New Orleans, we've been fortunate.

Not the way *he's* been, mind you, with a *Food Network* cooking show and a travel schedule racing between his huge, glitzy restaurants in Vegas, Orlando and South Beach. But we *have* been fortunate, in our own, small way.

"Little Clete Baldwin," Meridyth exhaled at last, looking up at me in a careless way once she was seated against the wall, a paid protector balanced on either side.

"It's Brett," I said. And when she looked puzzled, "I go by Brett now. Clete was my Daddy. And I don't exactly relish the association."

It was a familiar speech, and a not terribly pleasant one—but one that, in small-town Texas, I had to make often.

"I see."

Meridyth gave the matter a moment's thought, then opened into the smile I knew from all those magazine covers—which, come to think of it, was pretty much the smile I knew from that football Friday night long ago.

"Well, Brett Baldwin. The *halfback*. As I live and breathe."

There was plenty in addition to living and breathing I was feeling by this point. But what I said was what I always say in times of extreme eloquence.

"I think," I stuttered, looking down at one boot then, for variety, the other, "they need me in the kitchen."

I wish I could tell you I went back and fixed Meridyth Morgan the one dinner she'd never forget, no small order since she pronounced herself a strict vegan and wanted only steamed vegetables. I wish I could tell you my cooking changed her life, brought her to religion, made her beg to have my children—or at least to follow her back to LA, where she'd have a line of investors waiting for our Gulfstream with their checkbooks hanging open.

That last thing would have impressed me not at all. I'd already spent nine years as head R&D chef for a Houston-based restaurant corporation that was multi-national, multi-unit, multi-concept, and multi-just-about everything-else.

In the dark days after my divorce, when the vice president of operations suggested I might like to take a little time off, I told him, "I'll go you one better." As happens so often in this life, I understood in that difficult moment what I'd known I was going to do all along.

When I first moved home in late 2007, the coolest thing about Marfa was that its elevation was more than twice its population. I liked that Marfa's 2,121 people lived at 5,200 feet above sea level.

Actually, I liked a lot of things about my new/old hometown. There *were* a lot more transplants, for one thing, mostly from Houston, Dallas and Austin, but also from far-flung places like Denver, New York and Los Angeles. Oddly, the Marfa natives welcomed the transplants, even the Yankees. They drew some bizarre inspiration from the new people's rush to reinvent themselves. Before long, the natives started reinventing themselves too.

The renovated building on Oak Street near the Public Library that today houses Mesquite was Maria's Mexican Café for going on 40 years. My father took me there often when I was a kid, its one spartan dining room a swirl of ranchers like us, lawyers stepping over from Presidio County's peach-and-cream wedding cake of a courthouse, and a mix of jailers, county deputies, state troopers and dust-covered agents with the Border Patrol.

Originally, I learned, the building was a residence belonging to a man named Henderson who raised cattle down near the border. At some point in the 1890s, Henderson decided to move his wife and three daughters into town, so he started a bank to justify it. And he built his family a large adobe home that filled most of its city block.

The Crash of '29 did away with Henderson Bank along with so many others, and the Hendersons disappeared from all records I could find. The house sat empty for decades, all the way into the 1950s. At that point Maria took it over, did the bare minimum of repairs, and made it a viable business. When I inherited the building, I recognized the perfect use for all that "other people's money" I'd been offered in Houston.

As envisioned by a nose-ringed, seemingly 16-year-old architect from Austin, Maria's single large dining room became three smaller ones for a total of 80 seats, with a long and oh-so-stylish bar along the new glass front facing Oak Street. I ripped out Maria's tiny, grimy kitchen to make room for a bottle-lined 10-seat Wine Room, and added my own spacious stainless-steel cooking space in back.

Behind that, I planted a vegetable garden surrounded by a stone wall. In winter I can pick turnips, broccoli, cauliflower and artichokes, in summer sweet peppers and heirloom tomatoes. There are always fresh herbs for my cooks to snip. I feel happy every time I look up from my garden and see the town's shiny silver water tower looming above me, inscribed simply MARFA. Not "Home of the Shorthorns." Not "Named After Somebody in a Dostoevsky Novel." Not even, "We've Got More Art Galleries Than Feed Stores."

No, simply MARFA. Around here, you have to fill in your own blanks. And we prefer it that way.

Mesquite opened in the fall of 2008, and within four months Pat Sharpe was singing our praises in *Texas Monthly*. It wasn't long before John Mariani of *Esquire* came calling: he made us one of *Esquire*'s best new American restaurants of 2009. And *Food and Wine* stuck my smiling mug on their cover four months later, naming me one of their Best New Chefs.

The investors loved Mesquite, and not just for the media adulation or the dividends I was able to throw their way. Most of all, they loved having "their place" in hip/cool/cached Marfa, a restaurant they could bring their clients, wives and kids, and of course their mistresses. All were shuttled out in their private planes, preferably not at the same time.

The only guy in this thing without a private plane was me. But more than any of them, I got exactly what I wanted.

So...

The next time your life seems perfect—or at least good and safe and predictable—you need to be ready to work to keep it that way. Especially when a gorgeous movie star from your buried past sits at your table and starts changing everything.

MERIDYTH MORGAN MADE UP in alcohol what she lacked in sustenance. Two of our bartender's citrusy martinis cleared the way for a delicate Sancerre from the Loire Valley and then, to accompany the red meat she wasn't having, a dense and dusky merlot from Napa that seemed to have a cabernet somewhere in the woodpile. When a dinner of steamed vegetables lasts three hours, it takes no genius to do the wine math.

"Hey, bub."

The words, delivered with a hard edge by Meridyth's bodyguard standing inside my kitchen doors, cut through my focus on post-service paperwork: translating the notes, complaints, lame excuses, codes and hieroglyphics from my sous chef Gilberto Cruz as well as from Jaime, Jose

(Primero and Segundo), Arnaldo, Ernesto, Pepe, Paco, Manuelita and El Gordo into action steps for the morning crew.

It's hell when you're the only one in your kitchen who speaks English as a *first* language.

My system—some days the only thing that got me from one end of the day to the other—was a highly personal blend of over-organization and surrender to the void. Everybody stuck everything in this one big folder, which made sure that folder disintegrated on a regular basis. Each day (or night), I carefully went through what my staff had put in, pressing the pieces onward from there into one of 12 color-coded files, meaning one for each day of the week and the rest for specific subjects. Days off requests, insurance claims, internal disputes, you get the idea.

Only I knew what each color stood for. Only I needed to know. My filing system was one of those little things I relied on to hold back the chaos all around us. It worked, usually.

To hear me tell it sometimes, that long-ago case of "Friday Night Lights" was the first and only time I saw Meridyth Morgan. But we went to the same high school, a small one at that, even counting the invisible but uncrossable barrier between juniors and freshmen. I'd seen her around the hallways between classes, maybe in the lunchroom (though we ate at different times), and surely practicing with the cheerleaders as I ran through my afternoon drills with the football team.

And then, after we smiled at each other that night on the field, I saw her at the holiday formal a few nights later. That was hardly an accident.

Looking back on that night just before Christmas, as with so many other things in my life, I have to wonder: *What* was I thinking? I went to the dance without a date—thinking that act would seem tough, rather than any of the things it really was—and quickly scoped out the gym for that special girl with the smile.

The place was deafening, song smashing into song played by a DJ on a makeshift stage, the floor packed with young, uncomfortably dressed-up bodies swaying and throbbing to the beat. I found Meridyth eventually. She was dancing in a small circle of boys and girls, laughing, her eyes flashing in the spinning colors and lights.

Freshmen, I thought.

Pushing through the crowd that surrounded her, issuing "Excuse me's" that no one could begin to hear, I carved my way into Meridyth's circle as the other dancers pulled back to create a pool of light. I stepped in and, with all my well-rehearsed confidence, asked Meridyth to dance with me.

"What?" she shouted.

A lot of women over a lot of years have asked me that very question.

I repeated my invitation, but she only shrugged and brushed an ear with her hand. It was as though we were all deaf. And honestly, to this day, we're pretty lucky we're not.

"What?" she screamed again.

I gathered my courage around me and pressed my lips next to her ear. I issued my invitation one more time—and she nodded, understanding at last. Since she was only a freshman, I figured she needed a moment to get her excitement under control.

Meridyth shouted something to me then, during a particularly thunderous stretch of noise, and this was my turn not to hear. I smiled and shrugged, thinking it extremely irresistible that I mimicked her. We, I decided, were practically a couple already.

She nodded to me, then around to her friends, and finally to one tall farm boy in particular. Meridyth moved close enough for me to touch her, to embrace her, to kiss her. As the music dropped without warning into a deep well of silence, she cupped her two hands around my left ear and shouted "I'm with him!"

As you can see, I've forgotten the incident entirely.

"Hey Baldwin," the bodyguard said, breaking into my memory of Meridyth a bit too sternly. "She'll see you now."

As a general rule, I'm not one of those chefs who loves to visit tables.

Sometimes I have to, when a big-spending regular wants to ask me for something special: you know, the salmon he caught on a light fly rod in Alaska nine hours ago that he bought an extra first-class seat to fly down to West Texas. Those guys always get your attention somehow, and you push your real cooks to the side with a shared curse and start calling for stuff that only they know where it is anyway. Besides, you probably shouldn't do very much to a salmon that flies from Alaska first-class.

"All right," I said, piling the papers of different sizes with different things spilled on them into my manila folder and flipping the cover shut. "But hold on a minute."

I stepped into the pantry that doubled as my changing room, reaching for the immaculate chef's jacket hanging just inside with my name embroidered above the pocket. For some reason, I stopped in mid-reach. Except that I knew the reason. There was a mirror on the back of the door and I'd just caught the quickest glimpse at the face that launched a thousand plates.

I was tall, though not as tall as my Daddy, the leveling influence of my mother. And years of lifting full stockpots had built my chest, shoulders and arms in a way no fitness center ever could. There was considerable stubble on my chin, a result of TX function rather than LA fashion. Stubble is what happens when your nights collide with your days, with neither time nor place to do anything about it.

My eyes stared out from beneath dirty blond ringlets—no, I don't mean dirty blond the color; I mean dirty blond the condition—and, for all the thoughtfulness I brought to such a meaningless task, I decided I looked tired. Old and tired. At 38 years old, that couldn't be a good thing.

I stared harder, into the mirror and beyond. And then I remembered.

As I'd walked away from Meridyth all those years ago, my steps fast and deliberate, it was all I could do not to break into a sprint. My face felt like it was on fire. I turned away from anyone I recognized, for fear they'd need only one glance to know the whole story.

"Hey Clete!" my best friend Ernie shouted from where he was dancing with his girlfriend. But I held up my hand as though to block his voice and rushed for the nearest exit. By the time the icy December air outside slapped my face, I had to stop. My breathing was tortured, and I felt dizzy.

I bent over, hands on my knees, eyes shut tight against whatever heat singed them at the corners only to turn cold in long lines down my cheek.

"Clete!"

"Jesus Christ!" I snarled before I could open my eyes, before I really even listened, not even struggling to lift my head. "Can't you damn people ever just leave—"

And I stopped. Then, in fact, everything stopped. It was Meridyth standing there, her expression caught between the remnants of a warm smile and a fresh indecision flirting with fear.

"Oh," I said. "I thought—"

"I know," she said. "Really, it's okay."

I turned my head to the side, using my hand to quickly clear my cheeks of whatever might have gotten on them somehow.

"Geez," I mumbled, "now I'm really embarrassed."

"You don't have to be."

"Easy for you to say."

"I mean, come on. All you did was ask a girl to dance."

"A real pretty girl at that."

"Oh stop," she said, not meaning it.

"It's true."

"Well, I guess my mother would be happy to hear it."

We laughed, and it didn't take too much effort to believe we were laughing together.

"I'm sorry about what happened in there," Meridyth said, lowering her voice as she moved closer. I caught myself checking over my shoulder, making sure no one was watching.

"It was loud, I guess," I said.

"Yes, that was it. It was loud. It made us shout, right? I mean, we could have just had a nice conversation. And talked about stuff. Like we're doing right now."

"Yes, like we're doing right now."

Meridyth stood almost touching me in the cold, and I realized that she'd left whatever coat she'd brought to the dance inside. Her arms and shoulders were bare above the ruffled top of her red dress. It slowly dawned on me, as I shook myself free of my usual self-absorption, that she was shivering.

"My God, Meridyth. You're gonna freeze to death." I started to peel off my jacket. "Here, you'd better—"

"Clete, listen. I've got to get back inside. You know." She nodded toward the door and, for the briefest moment, rolled her eyes. "I mean, I just have to. But I wasn't sure I'd find you, or where you'd gone, or anything. So I wrote you a note." She looked into my eyes. "You could help me out by not gloating, okay?"

"I'm not. I, um, really."

"So yes, I wrote you a note. And I was going to, well, I don't know, give it to your friend maybe, or stick it in your mailbox at home, or —"

"A note?" The word finally registered, and I felt a thrill unlike any I'd ever felt before. Or maybe since.

"It's not like some big long letter or whatever." She opened her hand to reveal a crumpled corner of an envelope. "Give me that hand of yours, sir, before I turn into a freaking iceberg out here."

Powerless, I offered my hand and she placed the paper carefully at its center. Fingers brushed fingers. There was a quick smile. And then she sprinted back to her boyfriend in the gym.

"Water Tower," I read in disbelief once I'd turned the note over. "Tomorrow Night. 10. M."

No one was at my house when I got there from the dance, carrying that torn piece of envelope like it was the Ten Commandments. I sat up in my father's chair for hours, waiting, hoping, *dying* to tell somebody my news. But when my mother finally came in, sometime after 3, she was crying so hard I couldn't say a word.

"Your father and I are getting a divorce," she announced deliberately, as though she'd been practicing the words all night. "You and I are moving to Houston." My mother looked like she was going to cry again, and I felt myself rise from my father's chair to comfort her. Instead, she just said, "Now."

I tore my gaze from the office mirror. I looked at the immaculate chef's jacket with my name embroidered on the pocket, then down at the splashed and splattered no-namer I had expedited in all night, and scowled in the direction of Meridyth's impatient bodyguard.

"Screw it," I said, more to myself than him. "Come on."

As I knew it would be, the dining room was empty by this hour, the only small sounds coming from Jaime's younger brother mopping the hardwood floors. I left the bodyguard in my tracks, turned a quick couple of corners and looked in on Meridyth Morgan the Hollywood star. It was as though, in some strange way, I was seeing her not again after more than 20 years but for the first time.

The alcohol had taken its toll, of course. Her posture had adopted an unbecoming slouch and her eyes a red-lined emptiness that no one should ever see—which meant the tabloids that chased Britney, Paris and Brangelina would pay big money to see it. Her clothes, the sort of jeans-casual Western pieces that cost a fortune to look like they don't, were shoved this way and that out of line, resembling in the glow of the table's sole candle a Rembrandt that Picasso had taken a few minutes to fix.

Still, somewhere in this skewed vision was the 14-year-old girl I'd seen that Friday night, bathed in all those stadium lights, and the smile that had promised so much for a future I never got around to. It took Meridyth a long time to look up and motion me into the seat across from her.

She seemed to study the half-empty coffee mugs left by her driver and bodyguard, then nodded for the two men to get lost. They didn't stick around to argue.

"I suppose," she said, her voice not as slurred or rough as I expected. Still, she *did* have to start over twice. "I suppose… you're wondering why I came here… tonight."

"Well, no, actually. Not usually." Something about her, maybe just the whole vulnerability thing that always works on guys like me, made me want to be less of an asshole. However, a freight train can't learn to stop on a dime. "Since you turned up your oh-so-famous nose at all 11 of my appetizers, 17 of my entrees and six of my desserts, I could be tempted sooner or later to ask myself that. So yes. I guess I am."

"I didn't come in here for dinner."

"In my own small way, I'll take that as a consolation."

"I came here to talk with you." I couldn't tell if she was dead serious, slightly ill, or simply drunk. It was as though her lips, her words, and especially her facial expressions, were a split-second out of sync, like a dubbed art film from Bulgaria. "To ask you something. To ask—" she looked down into her wine glass, lightly smudged along the rim with lipstick and at the bottom with a drop of Napa's finest, then back up at me—"to ask for your help."

The words got out before I could catch them: "Why me?"

Man, I really hate those words. I've hated them for years. Ever since a Catholic priest who befriended me during a bad time in New Orleans told me that's what the prophets in the Bible always said. You know, when they got the call. *Why me?* Usually I can stop myself before saying that, with very good reason. It never worked for Moses or any of those guys either.

Suddenly, she reached beside her leg, brought up a purse so small it couldn't hold anything and then, by my lights, reached through it into another dimension to retrieve a pack of cigarettes and a lighter.

"Do you mind if I smoke?

"The law does. But I don't much care. We're closed. So sure, go right ahead." I waved away the one she offered me. "Been there, done that."

I let Meridyth light her own cigarette, then watched as she shut her eyes through the longest drag on anything that glowed I've ever seen. It was drawn-out and intense enough to produce instant ash, which she flicked with concentration into the bowl of my $34 Riedel glass.

"You know," she said, "how this place is? This *town*, I mean?"

"Yeah?"

"You and I were kids here, and we know how it used to be. But we know how it is now too. And I… I can't just go to the sheriff with this. How long do you think? Two, maybe four hours, before we see him all badge and hat on Entertainment Tonight, telling them everything he doesn't begin to know? Right?"

"Sure. I guess.

"And now, oh God. With everything that's going on." She looked down at the table, catching my eyes only by accident. "And me trying to keep my son from being taken to Italy. And everything those scumbag lawyers are saying—"

"I can see I need to keep up."

She stopped, glanced at me uncertainly, then smiled. "Of course, Brett. You wouldn't keep up, would you? I've asked people about you, a *lot* of people, and I really should have known."

"So, Ms. Morgan, you—"

"It's Meridyth. Please. For you, it's Meridyth."

"So you want my help with something. If it's anything you oughta be asking me about, I'm sure I can help you. A party. A reception. Maybe catering a movie shoot. I mean, I've done all those things, in Houston and other places you probably wouldn't believe. I'm sure we can work something out."

"Brett." Meridyth stopped until she caught and held my eyes. "Do you remember Enrique?"

"Your kid brother?" She nodded, but I didn't really need her to. Enrique was somebody I was unlikely to forget, even though he was younger than she was, and therefore much younger than me. Eight or nine Enrique was when his name first turned up in the local paper, arrested for small acts of vandalism, mostly breaking stuff up around his school.

Fighting came next, and in West Texas it's got to be bad before anybody even *notices* fighting. Auto theft, I think, came next, or maybe the first of several drug possession arrests. Left to fill out the rap sheet on my own, I'd guess intent-to-distribute followed, but by that point I had left Marfa and wasn't in any mood to look back.

"He just got out of prison, you know."

Yes, *that* Enrique.

"Good news, yes?"

"Sure. That's why I bought the ranch."

"I thought you wanted to do big important things here, to make it like Telluride or Vail or whatever."

"We *can* do that here. We really can. But I only want to because of Enrique. I knew nobody around here would hire him—31 years old, with *his* prison record. And anyway, what would they hire him to *do?*"

"No time to develop useful skills, eh?" I offered her a smirk I really should trademark. "He probably should look into the restaurant business."

Meridyth seemed hurt at first, but then shook her head briskly, as though to clear it—if she was smart, she'd clear it of *me*—and then pushed ahead with her story.

"When Enrique was arrested, he was charged with being part of this drug operation based in Mexico."

"A cartel?"

"Exactly. But he was only part of it, you see, not even a big part. And that's always the way it works. They pick up the little fish to get to the big ones. This guy named Morales."

"I've heard of him."

"Victor Morales. He was who they really wanted, not Enrique. But my brother gave them nothing, you understand? He just sat there through his whole trial—I mean, I was filming in Spain, my first movie, very small budget, but this is what I was told. Gave them *nothing*. So of course they sentenced him to 45 years."

"And he's out now?"

"Exactly. After only seven." Meridyth let that number sink in. "'Don't worry,' is all he tells me in the phone call. 'My lawyer pulled some strings.' Don't worry. That's what he always tells me, every time I ask. About anything, really. I bought the ranch a year ago, when Jason Brookman went to prison. Kinda from the feds, since they'd seized the place in the drug bust, you know. Anyway, Enrique has been running it for me. Since Day One."

I tried to let this all sink in. To find a folder or folders where I could shove all these loose bits of paper. It's what I did, every day and every night. No, it's what I *do*. But something about these loose bits of paper didn't fit into any of my convenient folders.

"So, Meridyth. Your brother is running your ranch for you. You don't want me to cook anything for anybody. And there's something you don't want to tell the sheriff or the media." I clicked my index finger on the table, as though it were the business end of a pencil. "So 1. You don't need me. And 2, I probably know somebody in or around town who can help you with whatever it is you need."

"No, Brett, no. You don't understand at all." She spoke now with icy heat, the kind that can turn molten in an instant with fear, with passion, or with something else I couldn't begin to name. "*Please*, Brett. You *have* to help me. You're the only person here I can trust. I'm really scared. Enrique's mobile just goes to voicemail. And when I got here from New York this afternoon, the staff said he's been missing for five days."

THREE HOURS AFTER MERIDYTH let herself be supported out to her Hummer and driven westward beneath a starless night, I lay awake more troubled by Enrique's disappearance than I ought to be. It didn't help that three extra-loud Southern Pacific freight trains passed through Marfa in the darkness, one for each of the times I almost was going under.

First came the long, lonely whistle far away, then the dinging of crossing signals in stereo from all over town, and finally the chugging and wheezing of the train itself. Some folks, thinking about safety or somesuch, think trains should slow to about two miles an hour when they pass on through. But when you're sleepless and the slightest noise makes certain you stay that way, here and gone at about 95 sounds right.

The Enrique news struck a chord, I understood, but one that should have ceased reverberating so horrifically years earlier. When one of your parents has disappeared, I suppose that's just the way it works.

Big Clete Baldwin, dishonest rancher, heartless womanizer, absent father and all-round lousy human being, one and the same—he'd wandered off his ranch with a loaded shotgun one morning 12 years ago, telling his staff he was going to get himself some jackrabbits. Nobody ever heard a shot, and nobody found him or his body either. The sheriff and a whole army of staties agreed he couldn't have gotten far, the terrain being rugged and the season being summer. But he was gone.

I hadn't seen my father since the divorce, and being an angry teenager (what other kind do they make?), there was none of that initial pathetic letter-writing and phone-calling that might have happened at a tenderer age. No, I knew only that Big Clete was gone, from this earth it seemed, as certainly as he had been gone from my life for somewhere approaching forever. Still, I have to say now, the hole he left in me when he disappeared was more painful than any I would have ever expected. Or admitted.

After my father was declared dead by the courts, as much to keep the ranch from rotting away as anything else, it turned out he'd left the place to me. Which would have been fine, had that act made me slightly rich the way I figured it was supposed to.

Instead, my new bride and I discovered, there were so many liens against anything of value, so many disputes over property lines and mineral rights, and just so many problems costing money to figure out that, by the time I got any check from selling the ranch at all, there wasn't a whole lot left. It was just enough, barely, for me and Julie to make a downpayment on our small first house in a Houston suburb that she liked.

Julie still lives in that house, about an hour's worth of traffic and road construction from anyplace I ever could have gotten a decent chef's job. I guess it all worked out. Thanks, Dad. Thanks a lot.

"The hell?!" I shouted at nobody in the darkness. Which, of course, in

Texas is always a complete sentence.

Tossing the covers against the wall, I rolled out of bed, into my jeans and across the ink-black front porch between the lethal ocotillos and Spanish daggers to my dust-caked red Jeep Cherokee 4X4. On the way, I grabbed my cream-colored cowboy hat off the rack—my MLC, I call it, for "Marfa Low Crown," the style it goes by at Big Bend Saddlery in Alpine. I often slap it on to visit tables full of tourists at my restaurant. It makes the right West Texas statement, even though my mother would die seeing me wear any hat indoors.

Down the driveway I gunned the Jeep, throwing up dust and swerving out onto the old state highway that heads south toward the moonscapes of Big Bend. There's a reason this is the nation's least-visited national park: You can't get there from here. Or from anyplace else either.

My headlights carved a dusty tunnel through the dirt and rock, with only the brown-green stubs of cactus for accent. I trundled on mile after mile down that empty highway, wondering where all the stars had gone, toward the ranch where I'd grown up.

It was still in my life, you see, by one of those twists that happen to people sometimes. The house and a piece of my father's old ranch are now where my sort-of childhood friend Jud Garcia lives and raises bison—that's buffalo to you and me—for a very rich divorce lawyer up in Dallas. I don't know what it is about Texas. Everywhere else, the big money is in personal injury. In Texas, it's in divorce. Which I guess works out to pretty much the same thing.

Once I'd punched in the gate code between the two stone sentinels the lawyer had installed, the road that led in toward our old house was pure West Texas caliche—a kind of calcium deposit, holding together dust, rocks, gravel and maybe silt from rivers that ran through these parts a couple million years ago. There certainly weren't any rivers now. The road covered close to five miles off the state highway, and when you're held to what feels like one mile an hour by all the ruts and trenches, that seems to take days.

No one answered the door at the house, and a quick check through open windows in various rooms turned up nothing. As I sensed the purple darkness stumbling toward dawn, I knew where I would find Jud.

Anybody other than me walking in on Jud Garcia in that barn a hundred yards from the house might have feared some ancient blood rite. And he might have started taking those notions of human sacrifice kind of personally. Yet I knew from the low and gravely sounds emanating from my friend inside a circle of lit candles that he was only praying.

"Oooooom-aaahh-oowwwiee" is what I think he was saying.

Jud was wearing just a leather loincloth, but the combined girth of his stomach, oversized arms and ham-like upper legs would have covered any private parts anyway. An oil-black rifle and a long wooden staff rested atop his crossed legs. His deep reddish-brown skin, stretched across muscle, was streaked with paint, mostly quick and violent slashes plus a few symbols I couldn't understand even when he'd tried to explain them to me. And, from just above his closed and paint-shadowed eyes, two thick black braids cascaded down across his shoulders, an eagle feather bound into each one.

"Jesus Christ," I said, hearing my own echo from the barn's upper extremities. "Can't anybody get a cold Shiner around here?"

JUD GARCIA IS, TO QUOTE my father's old hunting buddy Sukie Ward, "the biggest goddamn Injun I ever did see." All my father's circle, in fact, saw the West Texas of my childhood as so overwhelmed by "spicks" and a smattering of "niggers" that I suppose Jud was getting off easy. It was clear that any humans white enough to be considered "us" formed an elite fraternity indeed.

Jud raised his right hand in silence, as he often did in my general direction. Yet he was not, despite the physical evidence, swearing to tell the truth, the whole truth and nothing but the truth. He was trying, in spite of my interruption, to complete his prayers. Or his thoughts. Or whatever the hell else went on behind those closed eyes, since I for one have never been able to understand.

There have been exactly two deep metaphysical conversations in The Long Saga of Brett and Jud, both constructed, as well they should be, around longnecks full of beer for me and hand-carved pipes full of vegetal matter for him. It's the vegetal matter that might, all traditions of Jud's people notwithstanding, have landed us both behind bars. But the conversations might have been worth it. What I remember of them.

My father having lacked any semblance of religious faith, what little I believe comes from my mother's Catholic catechism—a menu of prohibitions that don't so much hold water as, in my life, have the floor to themselves. The constant reminders not to steal, kill, commit adultery, say nasty things or covet help a fellow well enough in a world that seriously lacks roadmaps. You could certainly do worse.

But if my mother's catechism had little use for Jud's two big a's—animals and ancestors—those things were all over whatever it was he placed his faith in. And they, with no heaven or hell, no limbo or purgatory, all lived within commuting distance.

Citing the traditions of his people, Jud insisted that animals and ancestors were circling around us in spirit 24/7, filling the air above our heads and the earth beneath our feet. At least that's what I figure he was trying to say, especially since his people have labored to take better care of the natural world than mine ever have. It's too bad, in a way, that Jud and I only discuss these things when we're too wasted to discuss anything else. It would be interesting, at least once before I die, to hear how such ideas hold up when you're sober.

"Come," he said.

I looked up. Jud blocked all the candlelight, and I could see that my beer would have to wait. Covered in slashing black symbols against an undercoat of red-on-red, he used his rifle to motion us toward the barn door. We stepped outside into the beginnings of dawn.

"It's time," he said.

Following a path we'd traveled before, Jud and I worked our way up over a steep rise then slid down into a valley that had a few patches of green. I knew more than saw what color they were, since here the sun hadn't touched yet and the cactus was edged with moisture in the shadows. Inside a wooden pen with a metal gate, a gathering of large black shapes waited nearly motionless, only their rough cough-like breathing making them stand out from rocks or thick, squat bushes.

"You," Jud said. "Wait here."

He went in and shut the gate behind him, even as the light inside the pen began to change. Deep purple and blue no longer, it lightened into a cottony gray as the shapes became more individual, more recognizable. Jud moved silently among them, touching one here or there with the long wooden staff. Every four or five, he'd stop and study a while, looking deeply, eventually nodding as some decision was made.

By the time Jud removed himself from the group, he was chanting softly, under his breath but with resolution. He stuck his staff into the earth so it stood up stiff, a feather flapping from a knob at its top, and carefully raised the rifle to his left shoulder. He stopped chanting.

A single shot shattered the silence of the valley. And there in the center of that dark, shuffling herd, a bison fell straight to earth as though all four legs had been yanked from underneath it by unseen hands. None of the other animals moved. Chanting again, this time louder, Jud walked over and poured liquid from a vial into the thick purple blood pooling on top of the dirt.

"IT'S THE SAME DAMN THING," I said, slamming down my longneck and pushing Jud's pan-roasted bison filet into my mouth, followed by scrambled eggs with jalapenos and potatoes fried in bacon grease, followed by a rolled warm tortilla that acted as a kind of plunger.

"No way, white boy. You wouldn't understand."

"So you pour holy water on the blood of a bison you just blew away…"

"Harvested," Jud corrected, shifting in his chair to stretch out the street clothes he'd changed into. We were a long way from any street. "I harvested my brother so that we could eat. And it wasn't holy water. It was just water that's been prayed over."

I shrugged in surrender, starting another sequence with filet.

"See!" he said, waving his fork at my face. "You goddamn chefs are just jonesing to ruin my meat."

"Huarmph," I said, mid-potato.

"You all go off to culinary school for more money than I make working hard for five years, and you come back here and ruin my meat. Cook it fast, you'll say. Just sear the outside. But my brother here —" he looked down at the thick slices on his plate—"my brother wasn't placed on this earth to have his outside seared. He was placed on this earth to be *cooked*, slowly and lovingly."

When Jud goes culinary on you, it's hard to stop him.

Of course, chewing though meat that was tender without resembling marshmallow, with every chew releasing a gush of beefy-bisony flavor plus an aftertaste of fresh-cut grass, I and most other people liked it a lot when Jud went culinary.

The bison in question had been inspected by the state moments after hitting the dirt, poked and prodded by a little guy who drove over from Alpine in a truck not much bigger than he was.

Then the refrigerator truck from the processing plant backed into the pen, with seven Mexicans to help lift and guide the carcass inside. One of them operated a backhoe with a small crane attached, the guys wrapping a steel cable around the animal's hindquarters and letting it be raised slowly, with much grinding, overheating and many exhaled "cuidados" and "Aye ya ya's."

The blood got bad as the bison lost touch with the earth, sloshing and splashing out, forcing the Mexicans to jump back, as though someone above us were pouring it out in buckets. I walked away. I can break down a side of beef in my kitchen, quicker than most and with less waste, but I hate that part of a field harvest. The bison, I think, deserves better. And I said so at our breakfast. Again.

"White boy, you just don't get it, do you?" Whenever Jud gets on his "native people" jag, he sounds like the Lone Ranger's Tonto channeled through an older, slightly more cerebral Speedy Gonzales.

"My people lived here for a thousand years," he said. "More than a thousand. And they covered this earth from San Antonio, which wasn't even there yet, all the way west to here and beyond, and then south into the high mountain desert of Mexico. A huge area, you understand. And all we had to eat for a thousand years was bison. So the bison became our brothers."

"Sure," I said. "But you don't see me taking my veal chop to a family reunion."

"Because your people are shallow, and they have no respect. For *nothing*," he said, letting Speedy get a word in. "When you travel this earth with the bison, when his family and your family are one, you do not ride and drink and slaughter and laugh, leaving whatever you don't want to rot in the sun. You ask your brother's permission before you take his life."

"And the bison actually says *Yes* to this?"

"He does say Yes, because you are brothers. And when his spirit has been released, to feed you and your family, he stays close. A long time. Maybe forever. To watch as you draw life from his gift. That is why I sprinkle his blood with holy water, as you call it. And that is why I pray for his spirit, to thank him for being so generous."

"This is," I agreed with my mouth full, "being extremely generous."

Jud Garcia and I were raised without bison on the ranch, but we were certainly raised as brothers—as much as time and place and unrelenting human stupidity would allow. He came to us as part of the Garcia family, a little boy who even then wasn't little, when they slid off a mud-caked flatbed to work for my father.

As he often did in such situations, my father kept Senor Garcia far away, riding the edges of our land, and Senora Garcia extremely close. Eventually, Senor beat the daylights out of Senora and came gunning for my father. The Mexican was dead drunk, naturally, and then merely dead. I never knew where his body went, or where Senora and her two babies went either. But Jud stayed on, 10 or 11 years old at the time, a member of our extended ranch family.

Of course, he wasn't really a Garcia. They'd found him wandering in the desert, living off lizards and cactus, whatever he could find. They said it was a year or two before he even spoke, but then he quickly picked up Spanish and eventually better English than most other folks on our ranch ever did.

Jud was fluent in many languages now, including several of his own creation. Even the nuns who came in to teach us couldn't break him of this habit, any more than they could stop him from being left-handed. Both things, they implied, had something to do with Satan.

Jud cleared away the dishes and I opened a third beer to salute the morning, now getting on toward 10. Jud grabbed his pipe and stuffed in something that wasn't totally illegal and we headed into the living room of what had been my childhood home.

Back then, my parents called this the "sleeping porch," the place they threw down cots for any relatives or friends who turned up drunk or broke or running from the law. Over the years and three owners, the screen had been replaced by glass. And as the original interior space got transformed into Jud's weaponry and reloading room, the sleeping porch became his living room.

Jud got his pipe going. I finally could bring up what I'd come all the way out here to discuss.

"Hmm," he said, nodding thoughtfully. "Enrique Morgan."

"Yeah. Know him?"

"Much as anybody around here. Damn punk is what he is. Oughta still be in prison."

"So why isn't he?"

He shrugged, grinning so tightly that most people wouldn't notice. "I don't know nothin' 'bout birthin' no paroles."

"You think he *spilled* on somebody?"

"Not if he's smart." Jud briefly considered the possibility that somebody caught as many times as Enrique might be smart. "Not if he really worked for Morales, they way they all say."

"Bad guy?"

"Absolutely."

"So, what the hell is he doing out? You think they found new evidence? Something that cleared him?"

"Man oh *man,*" Jud shook his head. "You *have* been talking to that good-lookin' sister of his. Maybe she shudda gone before the judge at sentencing, to get *him* thinking' with what you're thinkin' with right now."

I took a swig of my beer. "Case dismissed!" I laughed, banging the longneck down like a gavel.

"Yes sir. Case dismissed." He set his pipe aside on what had been my mother's coffee table—yes, three owners later. "Listen, chico. Enrique is a very bad man. That's what Morales was likin' about him. And he was on his way up in the cartel when he was arrested. Definitely. There were rumors, you know. Not just drugs, but whatever Morales wanted. Kidnapping for ransom. Trucks full of illegals comin' across. Some of 'em dyin' out there in the heat."

"I remember that case."

"Chico, you name it. If Morales wanted in on something, Enrique got him in on it. And where I come from, that makes him a very bad guy."

That was when I noticed my mobile vibrating in my pocket, and I had a sudden bad feeling it had been doing so for quite some time. When you own a restaurant, you have to be reachable at any hour—if nothing else, to go bail your dishwasher out of jail. But you dread it ringing. You dread what you might have to do. You dread what somebody might tell you. All in all, I figure it's a lot like having teenagers.

I didn't recognize the number.

"Brett Baldwin," I answered.

"Boy, where the hell have you been?"

Johnny Lee Crow. Our new Presidio County sheriff. Little Johnny Lee, to be precise. Big Johnny Lee was our old sheriff. In my part of Texas, folks like to keep things in the family.

"I said, where the hell *are* you?"

"At the ranch." Anybody from around here would know which ranch I meant. "Is there a problem?"

You've got to understand: there's *always* a problem. Most of them, in the restaurant business, involve the people you count on and therefore try to keep free, upright and on your payroll. Anything else, any other incident or result, means trouble you really don't need.

"Baldwin, you need to get *out* here. There's been a fire."

I let that sink in for moment. It's what you always fear, yet it's also why you roll your eyes and laugh bitterly, like stroking a rabbit's foot, whenever your phone goes off. You say no way. Not mine. Not today.

"Where'd it start?" I asked Johnny Lee. "The kitchen?" Fires always start in the kitchen.

"Boy, what the hell are you talking about?"

"My restaurant -"

"Shit. You don't understand at all." Why are people always telling me that? "I ain't at your restaurant. I'm way out at your pretty little girlfriend's mansion. The one they say you spent the night with —"

"Meridyth?"

"Good. He remembers their damn names."

"She was at my *restaurant,* Johnny Lee." I struggled to form the words. "Is she okay?"

"Probably. But we ain't got a condition on her yet."

"Burns?"

"Some."

"Jesus."

"Plus two crispies here at the house. Kinda wondered, the way I do, why they didn't just get out once the fire was going."

"Well—"

"Turns out they were dumb enough to get their throats cut first."

"My God."

"So I think you better get out here, cuz you was the last person anybody saw with her. And I got a whole buncha questions. Or I just might start thinkin' you had somethin' to do with this."

"You know I didn't, Johnny Lee."

"Yeah, I do. But unless you get your butt out here, I might start thinkin' it."

After a couple more all-business exchanges, I snapped the phone shut and stood there in the house where I grew up, on the sleeping porch where I'd spent a variety of nights for a great variety of reasons. Jud was looking at me, sometimes like a question and sometimes like an answer.

"You know what this means, don't you?" he said.

"No. What?"

Jud drew a long breath, then let it out in short, slow chapters. "This damn thing has Enrique written all over it. And, well, what is it you yuppie white-boy college shits always say?" He fixed me with a cold, hard stare. "It looks like he's takin' it to the next level."

"SHIT, BOY," SAID JOHNNY LEE CROW, squatting on the coals like Gunga Din in hell. "You might as well take a good look. Probably more money than *you'll* ever see gone up in smoke."

The sheriff was almost certainly right, considering the amount of black and gray smoke drifting east on the breeze. But a lot of steel and stone remained of Meridyth's 12,800-square-foot mansion in the foothills of the Chinati Mountains. As it turns out, much of the original stone house she'd bought—or rather, that the dot-com zillionaire with the drug habit had bought from the heirs of Jon and Maria Zinger—still stood, with fire damage concentrated in a new section that may have hours earlier resembled a suburban mega-church.

The air was alive with cracking and popping. Huge pieces of steel had wrapped around each other in the heat, with mounds of red-hot bricks positioned as though for a luau.

"Started in the new section?" I asked.

"That's what it looks like."

"You remember the old Zinger ranch, don't you?"

"Sure. Came out here with my Daddy a few times. Quiet down some drunk Mexicans, that sorta thing."

"The Zingers wouldn'ta recognized the place, with all this."

Johnny Lee glanced at the charred hunks of steel and brick, then back at the surviving old section of the house. "Well," he said without energy, "they might recognize it now."

The sheriff rose from his quarterback squat and put his hands on his hips, straightening to his full 6-2 to suck in some fresh air. He glanced around, letting his gaze focus on the dry dessert valley, rising into low brown hills, with stark lunar mountains lifting upward in the distance as though pressed from the center of the earth.

"Come on. Might as well see about these guys." Johnny Lee led me over to what might have been two large blackened cigars, without angles or extremities. "Maybe you've seen them before?"

In their present form, no. But as I studied the bodies burned to charcoal, I slowly recognized the pieces of Meridyth's driver, the cowboy who had to be from New Jersey, and her bodyguard, the guy who obviously hated to ever leave the gym. There wasn't much left of them. I could see why Johnny Lee hadn't initially noticed their slit throats.

"Yep," I said. "Never got their names. But they worked for Meridyth Morgan."

"Well, on that note…" said Johnny Lee. "You might tell your faithful redskin over yonder you need to sit with me for a bit and answer some questions."

"Sure."

"He wasn't with you last night, was he?"

"No."

"Good."

I nodded at Jud, who stood by my Cherokee looking over the mansion's wreckage. His lips were moving, and I think he was saying his prayers for the dead. Jud nodded in my direction, without raising his closed eyes. Johnny Lee and I walked to his squad car, he slipping in behind the wheel and me circling to the passenger side.

"Aw shit," he said, squinting into the sun, which had just started to dip from straight overhead. He pulled down his visor, which didn't help much, and turned to me. "So tell me, what the hell do you know about all this?"

I told him, beginning with Meridyth's visit to my restaurant, continuing through her three-hour vegan dinner and ending with our conversation about Enrique. He listened straight through, squinting out through the windshield. It was nearly a minute after I finished that he spoke.

"She asked your help?"

"Yes."

"Why'd she need help?"

"Something to do with her brother."

"Why *you?*" I half-expected to see him grinning, the way he would have if we were still in high school. Johnny Lee wasn't grinning.

"I guess I don't know," I said, honestly. But I was increasingly interested in finding out.

Johnny Lee thought about that, then slapped his hands angrily on the steering wheel and flung himself against his door, hard enough to open it and let him roll out. He took a dozen long steps away from the squad car, pulling up against a low-lying mesquite fence that ran east to west till it disappeared into a deep gully.

Positioning his boot on the bottom rail, the sheriff swept off his Stetson and used his sleeve to wipe the sweat from his forehead. He stood motionless, gazing south, until he heard me edge up behind him.

"You ever think," he said, nodding toward the purplish horizon, "they're all sittin' over there laughing at us?"

"Who?"

"Victor Morales. Enrique. All of 'em. Across the border."

"You think Enrique's over there."

"*You'd* be, wouldn't you? After doing something like this. He always worked for Morales, from when he was a kid. He'd go back, even after what he musta done to get out."

"Enrique rolled on somebody?"

"Either that or agreed to give them somebody."

"But who?"

Johnny Lee shrugged.

"If he sold out Morales, you'd think he'd want to be running the other way."

"That's what you'd think, right?" Johnny Lee looked down at his raised boot, then bent over to brush some gray-black dust from what remained of Meridyth's house. "That's what anybody would think. But there's a lot about this I don't understand. This attack, for starters."

"I don't see why —"

"Shit boy, there's a why, all right. Probably more than one why. Maybe Morales made him do it. We can't rule that out. Or maybe he was after something he left here, and it just went wrong. Or maybe —"

"What?"

"Maybe that big sister of his isn't so innocent."

"She's in the *hospital,* Johnny Lee. With burns all over her."

"Yeah, I know. But you see some weird shit when you do what I do." He sighed deeply, still staring past the end of the mesa. "More weird shit every day."

I stepped up to the fence and draped my arms over the top of it, joining Johnny Lee in his gaze, picking out the violent crags that signaled the volcanic path of the Rio Grande. There was nobody around that stretch of river 23 hours out of 24 each day, I knew from camping and rafting there. But it was also the border between one nation and another, the barrier between the have-nots and a whole lot of have.

"You know," he said, "when you're born along this border and choose to keep livin' here, you think about one thing every day. You hear about what they have in Laredo or Brownsville, the gang wars, the kidnappings, the killings—you hear about all that and you tell yourself: That's there, not here. That's in a city. That's on a major highway. That's everything that can't touch us here."

"So —"

"So you marry a nice girl, have a few kids, maybe put away a couple of bucks. If you're lucky, the kids go away eventually, you and the wife knock back margaritas, have a few laughs before you're through. But every single day, the one thing you tell yourself is that the crap over there ain't ever gonna happen here."

"It's a good life, right? I'd say you have a pretty good life."

Johnny Lee breathed, not answering. Then finally, turning to face me, "Oh, and Brett. Can I ask you something? Serious, I mean."

"Sure."

For the first time, in the harsh sunlight above us, I noticed how lined his face had become. Tired. Older than his years. He moved his jaw almost painfully, chewing on something, even though there was nothing there.

"Do you think most people are good?"

"Where?" I asked, out of my element. "In the whole damn world?"

"Yeah. Anywhere. In general."

"Oh, like with statistics. I guess. Yeah, I do. Most people."

"And what about the rest of them?"

"The ones who aren't good?"

"Exactly."

"I guess that's where you come in, Johnny Lee. You know, the whole badge and gun, serve and protect thing."

"I'm only sheriff because my Daddy was sheriff. We both know that. Everybody in this county knows that. That's all, as best I can tell."

"I don't hear anybody complaining." I figured he'd probably keep the job as long as his father had. "And I think most of those people, you know, the ones who aren't good, are kept in line by the rules. Right and wrong. Legal and illegal. Going to prison. Dying. Fear, I guess. Yeah, it's fear, mostly."

Johnny Lee positioned his Stetson atop his sweat-shiny red hair so the brim draped his eyes in deep shadow. He was wearing a strange, tired grin.

"Sure, Brett," he said. "That's what does it. That's what holds everything together. But the thing I've been thinking about lately is this."

"What, Johnny Lee?"

He let out a long, jagged breath, as though each molecule of oxygen were a painful thing. "Did you ever wonder what would happen, really, if they *stopped* being afraid?"

AS JUD AND I AIMED THE CHEROKEE back toward town, before the first of three news helicopters buzzed past overhead, I had every intention of accepting Johnny Lee's parting gift of advice.

"You know what I'd do," he said, leaning in through my driver's-side window. "If I was you, I mean. A guy with a good set of smarts and a business doing pretty well?"

"What?"

He straightened up for a second, so I could see no higher than his badge as he scanned the still-empty horizon. Then his face was back down in my window. "I'd go back to that little ole restaurant of yours and try like hell to stay put. I'd slip on that clean white shirt and start making dinner for a buncha people."

Excellent advice, I figured. I hadn't gotten this far in life ignoring excellent advice.

It was going to be a busy night at Mesquite. It was my turn to come up with the dinner special. The way that works is, all day long, whenever I'm not thinking about something else, I'm thinking about what to make. Just sort of rolling ideas over in your mind, dreaming about things that might taste good together. It helps, I've found, to be hungry when you're doing it, as long as you're not choosing stuff merely out of desperation.

It also helps to know what's in your pantry, your walk-in cooler and your freezer. Nobody ever made a bundle in the restaurant business throwing away what was already bought and paid for.

"Jesus Christ!"

The first news copter startled me, sweeping in so low I could reach out and grab a skid. Thinking about specials—maybe chicken-fried steak au poivre, with a green peppercorn brandy sauce subbing for traditional Texas cream gravy—I hadn't noticed the copter until it was right above us, filling the upper half of my windshield.

"Some interest in the case, it seems," Jud said. I'm not sure where his mind had been for the opening miles of our drive. But it spent a lot of his time there. "This will be all over the networks, you know."

"Where was that one from?"

"El Paso, I think."

"I didn't see it enough to read it."

"They need a bigger number."

Thinking about specials was over. I could work a few things out when I got to the restaurant and checked in with Gilberto, going over what was what for the night, how many reservations we had on the books, and who among us in the kitchen and dining room was sick or incarcerated.

"You know, Brett, this is going to be huge. Johnny Lee is making sure of it."

"What the hell are you talking about?"

"He's already called in the FBI. And he's talking to Homeland Security."

"Those stupid people from the airport?"

Jud laughed, indulging my typical restaurant disassociation from everything most people think of as normal life. "Not exactly. The people who are supposed to protect us from terrorists, hurricanes, contaminated flu shots and probably crazed ice-cream trucks while they're in the neighborhood."

"None of that stuff is involved in this."

"Maybe. But that doesn't keep Johnny Lee from calling them in."

"Christ. It makes no damn sense, is all."

The second news copter buzzed us on its way up into the Chinati Mountains, this one all the way from Dallas, which is one heck of a long ride. It was barely half the shock as the first copter, though. How quickly we become accustomed.

"Jud, do you really think this is Enrique? I don't get it. I don't understand what he'd be after. With Meridyth, I mean."

"Seems to me, relying on the wisdom of my ancestors, that people start fires to hurt somebody or destroy something."

I thought about that.

"So Enrique disappears," I summarized, "or seems to disappear, from the ranch where he's been working. After being released from prison. After making, probably, some deal that's real bad news for somebody, who's presumably not in prison."

"Yet."

"Exactly."

"And his sister is Meridyth Morgan. Which is why this is news."

"Yes. So she's flies in to look for him. And then, on her first night back, her ranch burns down around her, killing two guys she's paying to protect her."

"Yep," Jud said, "that about covers it."

"But why?"

Nearing Marfa's outskirts, with just the courthouse spire and the water tower rising above the trees, we caught a glimpse of the third copter. I'd asked the big question, but I was having a lot of trouble coming up with any kind of answer. I figured Enrique was involved; there was just too much coincidence otherwise. In fact, it all seemed to revolve around Enrique. Without him, Meridyth wouldn't have been in that house—if indeed she was *supposed* to be when the flames started to swallow a few million bucks worth of steel, glass and stone.

"The FBI," Jud said, interrupting my thoughts.

"What?"

"They're arriving this afternoon. Johnny Lee is calling for a federal task force. To launch a manhunt for Enrique. And to investigate the links between the drug trade, illegal immigration and terrorism."

I looked at him, shaking my head in disbelief.

"How the hell do you redskins know these things? Smoke signals?"

"Better," he said, slapping a button on my console and letting the sound fill the cab. "Marfa Public Radio."

We got back to Marfa just about the time Food Shark was shutting down, so we took a place in the final desperate line for lunch. Anyplace else in Texas, a converted silver 1974 Ford delivery truck would be parked by a construction site and dishing up tacos and tortas to the Lone Star State's favorite labor force. Here in Marfa, Food Shark gets parked between an organic farmers market and an upscale bookstore—and it specializes in Mediterranean food.

At this point, though, I have to add: "Mediterranean" is what our culture now calls a handful of great foods that probably wouldn't sell if we more accurately dubbed them Middle Eastern, or even worse, "Arab." To me, Mediterranean means Cannes or Sorrento, not Amman or Damascus; but as usual, nobody asked me.

"Hey chef," Adam exuded from up in the Shark's ordering window, rounding out a long and busy lunch.

"Adam," I nodded, glancing around the cooking space inside. "You soloing today?"

"Yep. Krista's at a catering."

"And hey, I hear you guys are making house calls now."

"Oh, yeah. But only when it's slow. You do what you can, you know, chef."

"Damn right."

Adam wouldn't think of taking my money for lunch, anymore than I would the next time he and Krista came into Mesquite for dinner. The fact that today's lunch ran less than $30 for Jud and me, and their dinner with wine would push $250, in the business we're in, never enters the conversation.

Sitting at one of Food Shark's handful of angular, postmodern wooden picnic tables, Jud chomped down on a double order of shish kebab, while I opted for the Marfalafel—a local spin on falafel, chick peas gone to heaven by way of a deep-fat fryer, which is, of course, the traditional route. Both of us scooped up garlicky mounds of hummus on warm pita triangles in between bites of fatoush, the Lebanese vegetable salad with toasted pita croutons.

I knew how to make all these foods, of course—they weren't even hard to make. But when you're a fine-dining chef, everything you actually crave in this world tends to be served from a truck.

We arrived at Mesquite a little after four in the afternoon, pulling into the gravel lot behind the building and spotting the ranch hand who had come to give Jud a lift. He was leaning against his boss' hulking, gas-guzzling Ford F-350 pickup, with all the cares generally associated with hourly employees doing nothing on the clock. The man was positively beaming—as, I might add, was Jud's F-350.

"Oh," I said, "I always wondered what color it was. Or in this case, wasn't."

"Is that some kinda snide remark about it being black?"

"Exactly."

"Well." Jud's face took on an evil grin. "It's a black thing—you wouldn't understand."

"Neither would you, Redman." I nodded to the truck. "It's just, I thought maybe it was dust-colored. Or clay-colored. Or simply mud-colored."

"You gotta forgive my guy for doing such a good job," Jud said, hopping out. "He's still new."

Happily, Jud's glistening ride back to the ranch saved me another hour of driving.

"The sheriff's advice," my friend said, leaning his bulk into my Jeep through the open window. All the best people seemed to be doing that lately.

"Yeah?"

"Hombre, I suggest you take it."

"Sure," I said noncommitally, my mind already buried deep inside my kitchen.

As the night's special, I was still committed, in a loose sort of way, to chicken-fried steak au poivre. But when I stepped inside and saw Gilberto, my 4-foot-10, tightly muscled, hawk-beaked *indio* of a sous chef, haggling with one of our on-again, off-again fish guys from way over on the coast, all my previous bets were off.

There, buried in ice that filled the large wooden crate dripping and draining on my countertop, were six huge Gulf snapper, eyes as full and gills as red as if we were all standing on the dock.

"Jefe, buenos dias," Gilberto said in my direction, barely looking up from the fish.

"Good stuff?"

"Si, jefe."

"Fish tacos, maybe?"

"Aye muchacho," he said. "I have been thinking maybe so."

"Si, buy them." I nodded dismissively toward the salesman. "But don't let him screw us on the price. I'll make him come back and get them if he does."

"But," the salesman sputtered, "I drove all the way from Brownsville."

I smiled. "I always did enjoy that particular drive. You?"

There was no need to wait for his answer, having played bad cop to my sous chef's good. Gilberto would take care of us on the price.

As I unlocked the door to my tiny, hopelessly cluttered office, I began constructing the night's special in my head. Snapper fillets grilled over mesquite, with a light lime and cilantro marinade—just enough to infuse some extra flavor but not enough to make ceviche. Shredded red cabbage on each pair of corn tortillas, waiting for a piece of the char-striped fish and a pico de gallo of high-summer peaches that just came in from the Hill Country. A little more lime juice added at the end, balanced by a squirt of honey and a splash of Texas muscat canelli dessert wine. With minced jalapenos for heat. I wrote: Mesquite Grilled Snapper Tacos With Hill Country Peach Pico de Gallo.

Gilberto had every reason to smile. He was hoping there'd be some left for employee meal at the end of the night.

Having scribbled my prep and serving instructions for the tacos on a sheet of scratch paper—the back of some glossy sell-sheet for an industrial onion chopper—I launched myself into the stack of paperwork, including the manila folder from the night before. It seemed like a lifetime since I'd slammed the folder shut to go out for my command performance with Meridyth Morgan.

In the stack of rumpled papers, as expected, there were all the usual side orders of restaurant work: complaints about one guy not doing his job, about another showing up late or leaving early, requests for days off to visit family across the border, notations of shift trades that might or might not happen when the time came.

Most of these I'd turn into a schedule that got posted on the employee board, with a place for each employee to sign. It helped, I'd found, to put these guys on the record. Signing their name, for most, was the only writing in any language they ever did.

Stacks. That's how I operated, how I survived. In the beginning, there was chaos—that's how my Bible began each day. It was up to me to impose about 24 hours of order on each 24 hours of chaos. And then do it all over again. That's how it was that, when I lifted the final request for two days off onto the appropriate stack, I saw the sheet with the handwritten phone number lying underneath.

It was a cell phone number and I didn't recognize the area code. But I certainly recognized the words spelled out awkwardly just above the number:

ENRIQUE MORGAN

"Gilberto!" I shouted out my open office door. In an instant my sous chef was filling it. "You know anything about this note?"

Gilberto took the paper from me, studying it with immense seriousness but giving me no clue how much, if anything, the name or number meant to him.

"No, jefe. Do you want me to ask around?" He considered a moment. "It looks like nobody in the back wrote it. And it don't come from reservations." Brittany, the high-junior junior who answered our phone in the daytime, had much frillier handwriting. "You want me to check for you, jefe?"

"Yes. No. I don't know. I guess don't do anything right now."

Gilberto's tone changed, leaving behind the all-business Spanish-English for something deeper, perhaps even concerned.

"Is about the fire, isn't it, jefe? About that woman who was here?"

"You got me. It makes no sense."

"Maybe, jefe, this is a message from Enrique."

"You know him?"

"No, jefe. He's just somebody, you know, that's around. Families work for families, always. And families, jefe, they always talk."

"Okay Gilberto, what the hell are you saying? I'm not on some goddamn game show."

He smiled, shrugged a little. I wasn't sure how much he couldn't find the words to tell me—though his English was the best in the kitchen, after mine—and how much he just didn't want to. Or was afraid to.

"Jefe, like I say—I don't know this Enrique, except maybe to say buenos dias and mind my own business, you know. But I, well, I have this uncle who I think knows him, a little. They went to, you know, the jail together. Or met there. Or something, I'm not sure. But my uncle has been friends with, does a little business sometimes with—you know, just to get by the way a guy has to—"

"Your uncle does business with Enrique Morgan?"

"No, not him, jefe. My family doesn't talk about this, you understand. To me or to anybody. My uncle does know Enrique, because they were in the prison together. But the guy he does business with is Victor Morales."

Gilberto told me I could meet with his uncle—he could arrange it for the morning, if I thought it would help. Help? Help who? Help with what?

"Sure," I said. "Call my cell with the time and place. And thanks."

"No problema, jefe."

My gratitude for Gilberto's information had nothing to do with knowing what any of it meant, and everything to do with the difficulty he'd had telling me. It was a sobering reminder that the typical restaurant worker fixing your fancy dinner, whether his face is white, black, brown or green, is seldom more than one relative removed from people who'd rob you, rape you or kill you for less than I'll charge you for dinner.

I replaced my chef's whites with street clothes, relocked my office door, and told Gilberto those grilled snapper tacos he loved were all his for the fixing. Tucking the phone number into my shirt pocket, I headed for the hospital to get some answers.

BY THE TIME I GOT TO THE BIG BEND Regional Medical Center in Alpine, I'd decided something more (or less) than my usual openness and honesty would be required.

"Hi darlin'," I said to the overweight, bespectacled post-teen at the front desk. "Sheila," I course-corrected, reading her nametag over the top of the desk. "I'm Brett Baldwin. Sheriff Crow from Presidio County sent me to check on Ms. Morgan."

"The sheriff sent you?"

"Absolutely."

She paged through some mysterious documents on a clipboard. By every appearance, they were as big a mystery to her as they were to me. "I don't see anything about this on my sheets."

"Of course you don't. The sheriff just now decided he needed this. For his investigation."

"I guess it'll be okay. I mean, like, you knew she was here. Deputy Crawford's up there anyway, keeping an eye on things."

"*Clay* Crawford?"

"None other."

"I went to high school with his sister Wendy."

"Really? I mean, I never knew her, of course. She was way older than me."

I feigned a little horror and hurt. "That's fine—rub it *in,* why don't you?"

"Nah, I didn't mean that. You're looking good for somebody your age." She stopped to make sure she hadn't insulted me all over again, then set down the clipboard and beamed. "Sure, Mr. Baldwin, you go on along that hall. As long as the sheriff sent you. Take a left past the nurse's station."

I smiled. "I'll try my best to hobble over there!"

My new best friend shook her head and giggled affectionately. God bless small-town America. As long as there is one to bless.

Happily for my own sense of truth, I actually *had* known Wendy Crawford in high school—though I was hardly the only guy in our class left happier by the encounter. For his part, kid brother Clay was one of those remarkable people who, under the wide brim of his hat and behind the badge and gun, still looked about eight years old.

Taller, for sure. And a tad pudgier since his marriage to Anita, a waitress at Conchita's. But Clay hadn't changed a lot since I used to sneak in whenever Wendy was babysitting him. We'd fix him a bag of microwave popcorn and leave him genuinely transfixed for hours in front of Nickelodeon.

"Hey Brett," he said, rising from the folding chair he'd placed at the entrance to a long, empty hallway. To confront me, I thought. But no, only to greet me.

"Clay, hey man. I mean, Deputy. How's that gorgeous sister of yours doing?"

"Still with the oil guy up in Oklahoma."

"Could be worse, I suppose."

Actually, for Clay Crawford, I supposed that anything *not* what he was doing in his hometown would be worse. He had the empty-but-delighted look of someone who took maybe two courses at Sul Ross in Alpine before deciding the whole higher learning thing wasn't for him. There's a grin you wear regularly when your job is fighting crime in a town that doesn't have any. Or at least *hadn't* had any. Until now.

"Sheriff sent me over to check on her."

"Really? I mean, I been wanting to question her myself. But the docs say she's still pretty out of it."

"So Clay, really." I paused. "Are you *supposed* to be asking her questions?"

"Well, no." He thought deeply for a moment, looking more than a little found out. "I guess that's why the sheriff sent you, huh?"

"Exactly." I grinned. "Now where's her room anyway?"

A skinny young Indian doctor looked up from Meridyth's chart when I pushed open the door and stepped inside. He studied me with curiosity and more than a little suspicion.

"Sheriff Crow," I said, having become a man of few words. Lies, mostly. "You know, ask her a few questions."

"Such a waste of time! I don't know what you hope to get from her that the others didn't."

"Others?"

"The FBI, of course. As far as I could tell, they learned nothing. Don't you understand that a patient on this much medication isn't going to be your star witness?"

"I see." Something told me the doctor was about to shoo me from the room entirely, and at that point even my lies wouldn't help. "I'm sure you're right, doctor. But I have to give it a try, you know. So I can tell the sheriff I did."

"You're wasting everybody's time." He looked down at the clipboard, letting his exasperation be more than clear enough. "But if that is what you must do, please do it in the next 15 minutes. At that time, I'm going to increase her medication so she can get a decent night's sleep. She is here to recover, in case you people keep forgetting that. You can stay then if you want to, but any conversation will be over."

"Thank you, doctor."

He left, pulling the door shut behind him, and I finally let myself look at Meridyth. She lay on her back beneath the sheets, deathly pale, gauze bandages covering the arms that hung down at her sides. Her hair was matted on her forehead and spread out at odd angles on the pillow. A couple of drips found their way into veins somewhere among all the bandages.

I pulled my chair close beside her. Now that I'd made it this far, I wasn't sure what I'd come here to accomplish.

"I hope to hell," she slurred, her eyes closed, the words as muffled as though she were speaking through cotton, "you brought me some of those steamed vegetables."

"Meridyth?"

"I told them I'm a vegan. They said, Sure, we can do chicken." A smile crept across her lips. "Several different ways, apparently."

"Texas says welcome home." I think she laughed until it hurt. Which was no time at all. "You can talk? The doctor said the FBI couldn't get a word out of you."

Meridyth broadened her smile, though the drugs made it crooked at one end. "Let's see, Brett—what is it that I do—for a living? Oh that's right, I *act!*" I could tell she was under the influence of something, and I was pretty sure that another time and place, I would have wanted to share some. "Didn't you see my last film? The one where I played the nun?"

She paused to see if I needed another clue. I did. "Who pretended to be a hooker for the CIA?" She giggled. "You know, I wasn't *half* as terrible as they all said."

I leaned close and caught the glimmer of her eyes opening. Keeping them that way seemed to require more energy than she possessed.

"Meridyth, I need to talk to you. And we don't have long. Before your doctor comes back."

She nodded.

"Everybody is looking for Enrique. They say he killed your driver and your bodyguard. That's murder. Plus the fire is attempted murder on you. They have everybody who owns a gun in Texas out looking to arrest him."

I watched her closely as I spoke. Tears started to form at the corners of her eyes, but otherwise she didn't budge. When she couldn't stand to listen anymore, she opened her eyes and reached out her hand, barely managing to lift her bundles of bandages up from the sheets.

"No!" She glared at me, more angry than sad. "They're not trying to arrest Enrique. They won't arrest him. They're trying to *kill* him. To make it all go away. They're going to kill him to shut him up."

"But why, Meridyth?"

She yanked her head to the side, facing the wall. She stared at nothing for moment, then spun back toward me, her face showing immense pain.

"You know he made a deal, yes?"

"To get out of prison?"

"Yes."

"So Victor Morales is after him?"

"No, Brett!, No, no, no!" She kept reaching her hand toward me till I finally took it carefully in mine, watching to see if the pressure hurt through her bandages. "Brett, listen to me. It isn't about what he did. It's about what he agreed to do. And he's only doing this to *help* people!"

"Help people?" I surprised myself with the sarcasm in my voice, and wished I knew better how to control it. "Give me a break, Meridyth. Guy goes to prison, makes a deal to get his sorry butt out. Be serious. Enrique isn't trying to help anybody except *Enrique* here. And the longer you refuse to understand that, the more danger I'm afraid you'll be in."

"Be quiet!" Tears drew furrows down Meridyth's cheeks and left glistening spots on her pillow. "Listen to me for once, okay? You said we didn't have very long."

She drew a deep, labored breath, wavering between pain and the onslaught of drugs. She was struggling to connect all the dots, the dots I needed connected every bit as much as she did.

"You've got it all wrong, Brett. All backward. The people doing this to Enrique, they're not who you think. They're dangerous. And they'll do anything. Look what they've done to *me!*"

Meridyth squeezed my hand, as though she knew there could be nothing else. "You need to help me, Brett. You need to find Enrique before they do."

"Before the sheriff? Before the FBI?"

"Brett, we have no time. There's no one else I trust. You have to do it. For me!"

Two impatient knocks at the door. One impatient doctor's face in the doorway. We knew our time was up. Whatever had passed between Meridyth and me in those minutes was all I'd have to work with. It wasn't enough, not by half, but it was all I was going to get.

The doctor shunted me aside as he moved to increase her drip. There was no amount of great acting that would keep Meridyth Morgan in control of her performance this time.

For one extremely paranoid instant, I even wondered what the doctor was doing to her, what he was pumping into her. To heal her. Or to kill her. But as I watched him plod through his procedures at her bedside, I determined he was not the enemy.

Enemies there were, though. Maybe a lot of them. And I still didn't have a clue who they were.

After the doctor left, I sat in the chair watching Meridyth sleep for more than an hour. Saying nothing, touching nothing, thinking nothing. Her gentle, almost soundless breathing had a way of calming mine as the minutes ticked away, until our breathing was the same. Finally, I brushed my hand lightly across the top of hers and went out past Deputy Crawford to my Cherokee in the darkness.

AFTER A PITIFUL EXCUSE FOR A night's sleep, I gave up around eight, brewed a pot of coffee in my home kitchen and took my second cup with me to the restaurant. It was Friday. I had a lot to do.

There was payroll to be gone over and signed so our bookkeeper could cut checks. There were work schedules to post for the following week, incorporating all those handwritten pleadings in that folder I never got around to. And, in the major what-was-I-thinking department, on Fridays we served lunch—just a little thing for our regulars, but something we'd become a bit known for.

Gilberto always came up with the lunch menu and oversaw its preparation, but he and the guys liked it when I put in a Friday morning appearance while they worked. Maybe they appreciated my deep qualities as a fellow human being. Or maybe it was just that my efforts produced paychecks.

After about an hour of paperwork and another cup of coffee, purveyors started showing up—the big guys with their refrigerated trucks decorated with all manner of food company logos and little guys in pickups who raised rabbits or grew heirloom tomatoes. I poked and prodded, sniffed and tasted, consulting with Gilberto when that made sense and buying what I figured we'd need to get through a busy Saturday dinner and an almost-as-busy Sunday brunch.

A wine salesman stopped by with some new malbecs from Argentina and carmeneres from Chile. Since my wine guy was out sick, I was forced to do the tasting myself.

Spitting each mouthful into what was left of my coffee, I ended up adding the wines to our list. Malbecs went especially well with our glorified cowboy cooking, most of all with any red meat striped on our mesquite grill.

I did cheat a little, though. A serious wine taster would insist we work through the vintages before any morning coffee could ruin our taste buds for the day. I'm serious about wine. I'm not *that* serious.

Gilberto's Uncle Gustavo had agreed to meet me and tell me as much as he could, and I'd gotten the time and place from a voicemail on my cell phone. I didn't know exactly what Gustavo could tell me. Even worse, I didn't know what I wanted or needed to know. I had to make another stop on the way, though, at the Marfa Public Library, hoping what I found there would give me something to talk with him about.

"Clete Baldwin," said a voice unexpectedly just inside the library's front door. "In the flesh."

What I said to the woman who addressed me was, "Oh hi, Lola Mae." What I thought was, "Oh crap, it's Lola Mae Crow."

Johnny Lee's sister.

The gal in charge, formidably occupying the desk in the REFERENCE & PERIODICALS department. Lola Mae was also the town's most often-quoted source of gossip.

"I don't see you in here much," she said, brushing a long white strand of hair back from its apparently familiar place in front of her eyes. "Or in church on Sundays either, if I'm not mistaken."

"Considering I don't think I've been in here since the seventh grade, I'm sure you're onto something, Lola Mae. And as for church on Sunday, you've got a good eye, I guess. It's an occupational hazard that goes by the name 'Sunday brunch.'"

"So, you're still cooking for a living?"

"Yes. Still. But I'm Brett Baldwin now." Why did I always have to explain this to people? Really, how famous do I have to get before Big Clete Baldwin is known as Brett Baldwin's father? "I've started going by my middle name."

"Hmm," she said, turning the idea around in her head as though she were Sigmund Freud hot on the trail of a sexy dream. "I don't think doing that ever occurred to Johnny Lee. But of course, he's pretty *proud* of his Daddy."

"Good for him," I said, not wanting to press the issue. "I mean, that's a great thing. Someday, maybe I'll have a boy who's a little bit proud of what I do."

"Cooking?"

Sometimes in this life, there are no adequate comebacks. Other times, the comebacks are entirely adequate but unacceptably obscene.

"Ha." I smiled, slapping every type of punctuation I could think of onto that chapter of our conversation. "That's a good one, Lola Mae. A real good one. Now, Ms. Librarian, can you please help me with something?"

"As God is my witness, I should not just help you but write up the event in the library bulletin. He who was lost has been found."

"My question is: old copies of the Sentinel. You keep them here, right?"

"Paper's been published since the 1920s. So yeah, it'd be a shame to throw 'em all away."

"So, you've got them here?"

"One way or the other." She relished my confusion. "After 2001, we have the entire archive online—full pages, stories and ads and all. Before that, we have the stacks of bound copies, quarterly, with a separate index. And back before 1973, we have it all on microfilm." She paused. "They may have invented that since the last time you were in here."

Lola Mae offered to come to the archives with me and help me find what I needed, but I shook my head and insisted I'd manage. I wanted to take my time, I said, browse through some things at my own speed.

"Well, call me if anything doesn't make sense," she said, a bit too eager to be all wrapped up in my business, if you ask me. Besides, by this stage in my dealings with Meridyth and Enrique, I'd be more likely to call if anything *did* make sense.

Initially, I'd thought I'd start with the most recent stories and work backwards. But that way, I realized, I'd constantly be reading references to things I didn't understand. The only way to make sense of things—though no way seemed very promising—was to go back to the beginning. To *some* beginning, anyway. Find an arbitrary beginning and jump in. Which is what I did with the Sentinel of Feb. 14, 1996. More than a decade ago, I noted, hoping to come up with some kind of timeline.

OFFICIALS FEAR ESCALATION
IN BORDER NARCOTICS RIVALRY

PRESIDIO, Texas (AP)—Officials with the U.S. Border Patrol said Thursday recent outbreaks of violence on both sides of the border are signs of a widening battle for control of illegal drugs entering the United States from Mexico.

Last week's gangland-style murder of longtime warlord Carlos Maceda,

71, was viewed as proof that one or more rival factions were pushing for a lead position in the narcotics business based around the Mexican town of Ojinaga across the border from Presidio.

Jim LaSalle, regional officer in charge of the Border Patrol, said that while several younger drug dealers seemed to be in contention, one figure increasingly mentioned by minor workers arrested in the enterprise was Victor Morales. No biographical data on Morales was available, except that he appeared to have risen to the top of the often-vicious heap created by the transfer of illegal drug operations to Texas from Florida and the bayous of south Louisiana.

"Beginning in the 1980s, the federal government stepped up its pressure on the DEA (Drug Enforcement Administration) and the Coast Guard to intercept more and more of these shipments," LaSalle said in an interview. "It was the 'war on drugs,' if you recall. And there were some major victories, especially with attempts to enter the U.S. by boat."

According to LaSalle, it was unclear whether Morales was involved in criminal activities in Florida or Louisiana, or got into the narcotics business later in Texas. He said the drugs Morales brings into the United States are produced in Colombia, then flown into remote ranches in the Mexican state of Chihuahua for delivery via Ojinaga.

Presidio and Brewster counties, where most of the recent smuggling activity has taken place on the U.S. side, cover a total of 10,026 square miles along an elbow of the Rio Grande about 250 miles southeast of El Paso. They have a combined population of less than 14,000 people.

The wire story spun through several paragraphs describing the discovery of Maceda's body on the banks of the river, in that spot little more than a slow-moving stream through tall grass, the only true green you can see for miles. The cause of death, authorities said, was two bullets fired at close range into the back of Maceda's head.

Ojinaga was the latest point along the border to be singled out for traffic by the Mexican cartels, I read. Early efforts to reproduce the initial success of drug movements via the Gulf of Mexico into Brownsville were quickly identified and shut down, using techniques perfected off the coasts of Florida and Louisiana.

The trade then moved inland to the Laredo area, hitting its stride there by the late 1990s. A busy border crossing proved excellent cover for the drug traffickers, and the same Interstate 35 that carried goods ushered in by the NAFTA trade agreement now carried marijuana, cocaine and heroin to users on the streets of San Antonio, Austin, Dallas and far beyond.

According to the article, the quieter, relatively remote setting of Ojinaga and its sister Texas town of Presidio caught most DEA and Border Patrol officials by surprise. The location had always seemed unlikely, they said—until they realized the cartels had learned to send their drug shipments with illegal immigrants who disappeared into the United States using American-registered cars and trucks.

I shut the bound volume and dug back into the Sentinel's index. Even though I'd still lived in Houston back then, I had an idea where I was going, or at least of the time period. The story from Aug. 4, 2000, still seven years before I moved home, was a major one, covered by the paper's staff beneath a banner stretched across the top of Page One. It was a story of the events that sent Enrique Morgan to prison.

18 ILLEGAL ALIENS DEAD IN ABANDONED TRUCK

Presidio County officials were meeting Monday to decide on their response to the discovery of 18 illegal Mexican immigrants found suffocated over the weekend in 100-degree heat on a deserted stretch of highway between Lajitas and Big Bend National Park.

One man was arrested in conjunction with the incident. He was identified by officials with the Drug Enforcement Administration as Enrique Morgan, 20, of the Marfa area. Morgan has an extensive record of arrests, mostly relating to smalltime narcotics distribution, officials said.

"It looks like a lot more people were in on this thing," said Harry Bowhalter of the DEA. "Something like this, crossing the border with people and narcotics in the back of a sealed tractor-trailer, required planning. But when we got the report of the stalled truck on the side of the old Lajitas highway, we went to the scene and found only Morgan and the 18 dead bodies."

Medical examinations were scheduled Monday for the victims, who were presumed to have suffocated in August temperatures that probably reached above 100 in the sealed trailer. There was no food, water or ventilations were the bodies were found.

Cocaine discovered in the trailer weighed more than a ton, officials said.

Morgan, identified as an associate of border drug lord Victor Morales and questioned as a 16-year-old in the execution-style killing of rival Carlos Maceda in 1996, appeared dazed and incoherent when he was taken into custody at the scene.

A hearing is scheduled Tuesday to file charges and consider bond. However, DEA officials said that, as murder or manslaughter charges may be included, prosecutors would likely ask the judge to refuse bond.

The world felt like it was spinning around me, more out of control than any chef allows it to ever be in his kitchen. I'd never known any of this, though the case had made national news. Still, seen from the comfort zone of my former life as a corporate chef and married man in a Houston suburb, it was only one of several incidents that summer involving illegal aliens dying from the heat.

Enrique had gone to prison as part of that case, though clearly no murder or manslaughter charges had stuck within his sentencing to 45 years—or, of course, his release after only seven. I read every word of the Sentinel's front-page story and then each of the many sidebars on inside pages, including one piece recycling the AP story about Morales and the escalating drug violence.

By the time I'd turned pages to a couple issues later, I was trolling so carefully through every headline that I caught the small one-column story at the bottom of an inside page.

CHURCH GROUPS
HOLD SERVICE
FOR UNBORN BOY

Members of Big Bend-area Protestant and Catholic congregations gathered Thursday evening at Grace Presbyterian Church to pray for an unborn child who raised the number of victims of the recent human-trafficking tragedy to 19.

Church leaders said the death of the seven-month-old male fetus, removed from the body of Maria Elena Salgado, 19, only made more clear the need to end human trafficking tied to the drug trade along the Mexico-Texas border.

Attendees were encouraged to send letters to their congressman in Washington, insisting on tougher enforcement of laws affecting illegal immigration. All trucks and other vehicles entering the United States should be inspected thoroughly before being allowed to pass, church leaders told the approximately 50 people who attended.

By this point, I could have fast-forwarded through the years and found the appropriate bound volume on the stack nearest the wall. But the last article I needed to track down, dated (it turned out) Feb. 26, 2008, was archived online, which meant switching tables to one holding a dusty-looking computer terminal.

The Sentinel and the Presidio County Public Library must know their readers pretty well. They made the system idiot-proof.

LOCAL CELEB'S
BROTHER GETS
EARLY PAROLE

Enrique Morgan, brother of Marfa-born Hollywood star Meridyth Morgan, is being released early from his 45-year federal prison term in the drug-and-human trafficking case that left 19 illegal aliens dead in an abandoned truck along the highway from Lajitas into Big Bend National Park.

Officials with the U.S. Justice Department refused to comment on Morgan's release, except to say it was a parole related to new information it had received about the case. They refused to elaborate on possible sources of that information.

"The tragedy involving those 19 deaths is an ongoing investigation," Kurt Steinman, spokesman for the Justice Department in Washington, said in a three-paragraph news release. "It is our policy not to discuss ongoing investigations."

Before his arrest at the scene of the deaths, initially reported as 18 but raised to 19 after one of the victims in the hot, airless trailer was determined to be pregnant, Morgan was considered a member of the dangerous Victor Morales drug cartel. He was questioned by the Drug Enforcement Administration at age 16 after the 1996 gangland slaying of Morales rival Carlos Maceda.

No charges were ever filed in that murder, considered at the time an effort by the Morales organization to show its power over all other groups involved in illegal activities along the border.

Meridyth Morgan, now a resident of Los Angeles and star of the recent hit film "Deadly Habits," in which she played a Catholic nun working for the CIA, could not be reached for comment. A spokesman for Constellation Films said she would issue a statement on her brother's parole within 24 hours.

I was halfway through that final sentence when I felt a dark presence behind me. Too close behind me. It was all I could do to calmly turn and gaze up into the emotionless eyes of Lola Mae Crow, reading the Sentinel on the computer screen over my shoulder.

"I think I've found everything I need," I said quickly, smiling with all the charm I could muster. I clicked on the archive to shut it down. "Wow, just look at the time!"

"Well," she said, strictly business, "you were being so quiet over here. I *only* wanted to see if I could help."

I spent a frenzied two minutes putting away the bound volumes I'd used, finding the order they needed to be in to attract the least attention. Lola Mae wasn't there when I walked past her desk. But then I heard whispering and spotted her standing in a tiny office behind the last bookcase before the stairs.

She was speaking nervously with someone on the phone, unless that was only my imagination. She looked up and covered her mouth with her hand as I raced by.

UNCLE GUS WAS WAITING. And he didn't look happy.

At the request of his sister's son, Gustavo Cruz had taken time out from his busy schedule of criminal activities. In crime, as apparently in all things, time is money.

All the way out of town to the deserted Marfa Lights Viewing Area, I'd had to work not to speed. Not only is there a latent James Dean in us all, especially when running late and faced with mile after mile of lonesome highway, but the articles I'd read at the library had filled me with a sense of unease, of disruption, I might even say of dread. Yet had you asked me at the time, I couldn't have told you why.

My commitment to the speeding laws of the Great State of Texas was helped along by two Highway Patrol cruisers strategically positioned along my route. Here in the western desert, there really isn't much to hide behind, so the forces of order tend to be waiting for you just over the hill. They *were* waiting, just like I knew Uncle Gus was. But I kept it legal, and the cruisers didn't budge in my wake.

Make no mistake: other than having some extremely basic information to ask Gustavo Cruz about, I didn't understand what I'd just read. I needed context. I needed more details. I needed something to help me connect all the dots.

Like most people who have relegated recreational drugs to a small, not very memorable corner of their youth, I found and find the whole notion of using drugs kind of boring. Therefore I knew next to nothing about them, what they did for you or what their nicknames were on the street, or how much money they sold for.

Of course, I was also aware that fortunes were being made moving drugs across the border. But, from my point of view, fortunes were also being lost—such as the one squandered by the jailed dot-comer who used to own Meridyth's ranch.

As a chef with the usual Tex-Mex kitchen crew and a young, painfully hip waitstaff, I was not so naive as to pretend illegal drugs were nowhere in my world, try as I might to be in charge of my personal reality. I'd learned as a busy line cook in New Orleans years ago that the fine white powder that kept guys pumping out 800 orders of pecan-crusted redfish and cochon de lait every night was neither sugar nor salt.

The archived news stories about drug smuggling and human trafficking had had the desired effect, I suppose. I was beginning to get some clue who or what I was up against. What I hoped to find out from Gustavo Cruz was why.

"I know you," Gus said by way of salutation.

Indeed, before I even reached him walking across the gravel from my Cherokee in a dust swirl on the side of the highway, he seemed to do a kind of double-take. He covered the look, that sense of recognition, quickly, since I presume in his business too much transparency is one of the long list of things that can get you killed.

"You know me?"

"Si, senor."

Gus ignored my outstretched hand, pretty much a mortal sin here in West Texas, and nodded me to join him leaning against the rock wall. We stood in silence in the overheated afternoon sunlight, gazing out across the scrubby desert made famous by the town of Marfa's only actual tourist attraction.

Sometimes at night, the sky above this flat, cactus-crusted, brown-and-bruise-purple lunar landscape fills with mysterious quivering lights. Over the years, these luminosities have been explained as distant car headlights or the cosmos passing gas—but also, of course, as our own Lone Star edition of UFOs. The folks who come out to this place for the Marfa Lights are, therefore, a strange mix of science nerds and substance-elevated biker hippies. Or, maybe that's not such a strange mix after all.

"I know you, Brett Baldwin," said Gus, focusing on me as much as he could when his eyes weren't nervously scanning the horizon. He at least, unlike the locals, called me by my chosen name. There were no other cars visible on the highway, only the burning sun and the roaring of the hot wind in our ears. "I know you because I've been to your restaurant."

"Really? I don't believe we've met."

Gus grinned, revealing a train wreck of yellow, rotted teeth that seemed at terrible odds with his clean American-made dress shirt tucked into jeans worn over an expensive pair of boots. "I never," he laughed, "come in by the front door."

"That's okay," I said, working to bond as best I could. "I never do either."

He shook his head, as though entertained by the irony of it all. Gus was two or three inches taller than Gilberto, which still left him a head shorter than me. He had dark *indio* skin and a thick, black mustache that covered his mouth completely when it was closed.

"It is Gilberto who call me," he explained, watching his boots slowly stir the gravel in ever-tightening circles. "When he need something. I can get, you know. From somewhere. Fish. Lamb. Those, how you say… *scallops?* You name it, Gus can get." He looked up, knowingly but not the least bit ashamed. Quite the opposite, I suspect. "He is my nephew. I think maybe he learn how a man operate, truly, eh? Without always telling the jefe, no?"

"Sure, Gus." I smiled. "Never tell the goddamn jefe."

"Claro. Is siempre, the same."

"Siempre," I said.

We stood without talking for a long time. In my corner of the known world, if you can't stand without talking for a long time, you're destined to live a very uncomfortable life.

"I am grateful," I said at last. "For you to see me."

Gus nodded.

"I was hoping you might help me. Might tell me some things."

He nodded again. What if, I wondered, all information from Gus came in the form of a nod?

"You see, Gus, I am trying to help someone, and she is in trouble. She and her brother, I think. And everywhere I look, everything I do, I keep coming up with—I keep, I mean, running into the name Victor Morales—"

"He," offered Gus, "is a powerful man."

"Yes, I gather that. And I do not wish to show disrespect to him, you understand? But I do not know why this is, that having barely heard of him before, he is now everywhere I look. Can you help me?"

"Victor Morales," Gus said, as though giving each word its own completed thought, "can be seen only when he wishes to be seen."

"But why? I don't get it."

"Ah, that's what Gilberto he say to me. He say you wish to ask me why,

74

why, why."

"Yes, senor. I do wish."

"You must understand, Brett Baldwin. I am not Victor Morales. I am only, how you say, a little guy. I do things, like for your restaurant. I work to feed my family. That is all. And I know only what I do, not what he does, okay?" It was my turn to nod. "But I know it is dangerous, what you are doing. With those people, your friends. They are not what you think. And you must stop now."

"Meridyth?" I heard my voice rise, not just in volume but in pitch. "I mean, give me a break—she acts in Hollywood movies, for Christ's sake!"

Gus shook his head, it seemed with sadness, as though the world was too heavy a burden for him to carry on his dark, slightly hunched shoulders.

"It is the border, you know? The border, senor. Not your pretty little world of rich gringos, eating and drinking and making babies in their, como se dice, comfortable houses. Not that world, senor. No. I promise you."

"Everybody is searching for Enrique," I said, not knowing how the ideas fit together. "To arrest him for two murders."

"Si. I know." He looked at me. "But on the border, they can look but sometimes cannot find. Because they don't *want* to find. As with Victor Morales. On the border, yes, of course—" he stopped, as though forming an idea that gave every sign of eluded him. "In this place, there are men in white hats and men in black hats, yes, like in your American movies. But every so often… just to make the movie impossible, you know… all the men, senor, they get together. And they exchange hats."

At that one, Gus had to smile. It had been a torturous act of translation, and he realized he had made it through.

"You wonder, Brett Baldwin, how Victor Morales can survive so long? With all your federales with their big guns and their spies, all trying to catch this very bad man, this villain? But here on the border, you must see, Victor Morales is not a villain. To all the people who have nothing, he is a hero."

"A drug dealer?"

"Yes, veramente. It is true. A hero. A protector. Like your, how you say, Robin Hood? Maybe a little of your John Wayne also. They are proud of him. They all want to be like Victor Morales, to live like him. To *have* his life. Look around you, now, senor. Seriously." Gus swept his hand across the desert, the nothingness that looked like a stage set for one long play about hopelessness. "Really, what else *can* they do?"

Gus' cell phone buzzed in his jeans pocket and he flipped it open on the way to his ear. Visibly shaken, he spoke three words in impenetrable Spanish—they always can, when they want to—then replaced the phone.

"I must go. That is my ride, you would say." Gus smiled, again that festival of nightmarish dentistry. "And I can tell you nada mas. Okay, is all, senor."

A barely civilianed military Humvee roared onto the gravel, managing to stop in a cloud of dust that the wind tossed into my eyes. Gustavo Cruz nodded, smiled once more and climbed inside.

Another time, another place, I would have watched the Humvee drive away, would have followed it with my eyes far off along the highway to the west. But it was at that moment that another vehicle rushed in from the opposite direction, this one bearing the seal of Presidio County on its doors. It must be a testament to the intensity of my conversation with Gustavo Cruz that I hadn't seen it coming a dozen miles away.

A screech. A driver's door exploding open. A snarling Johnny Lee Crow barreling toward me.

"You bastard!" he shouted. "You goddamn piece of shit!"

Before I could decide what to do—to run, to fight, to assume the fetal position—Johnny Lee was all over me, all swirling fists and feet. He shoved me first against the rock wall, hard and then harder, slicing my arms and my back through my shirt as I crumpled down its sharp gray-brown edges into the dust. He landed three punches to the side of my face on my way down, two more blocked by my forearms, then continued kicking any

76

body part that I couldn't close the rest of me around.

"You lying sack of horseshit!" He went on, variations on a theme. "You have no goddamn idea what you're into, do you, boy?" Kick. "Or who you're dealin' with." Kick. "Answer me, goddamn it. *Do you?*" My chest convulsed with each attack of his steel-toed boot, with more and worse pain each time.

I struggled to gather what little strength I had left as he threw himself on top of me in the dust, straddling me to hold me down in the shadow of the wall and heaving to catch his breath before unleashing the next barrage of punches.

"No, Johnny Lee," I sputtered, angry at last, feeling warm, thick rivers of blood running from my mouth and down my chin. "No, I sure as hell *don't* know. Why don't you just tell me, okay? You tell me, and then I'll goddamn know!"

"She's gone, you bastard. They came and took her. Because of *you!*"

"What the hell are you talking about? Who?"

"Your pretty little girlfriend is who. Goddamn Enrique shot his way into the hospital and took her."

"But." I had trouble finding the words, though I realized the days when words could protect me were going, going, gone. "She was—she had —all those burns."

"He took the whole goddamn thing, you retard. He took the doctor too. And just you wait. That greasy Ay-rab bastard'll turn up a body rotting in the desert in no time."

"Her doctor was from India," I said.

"Do you think I give one big shit where he goes to *church?*"

"Enrique shot his way? Into a hospital?"

"Yeah, and he's up to three now, you know that? Three! Your friend the deputy—whose big sister you used to bonk, the deputy of mine you were *lying* to all night? He's shot dead, goddamn you to hell. By one guy in a ski mask while two other guys held him down. Picture that, you stupid shit!

And him with a pregnant wife!"

Johnny Lee looked up into the sky, each shake of his head more violent, verging on more insane. "And if Enrique's thinkin' right now at all, he's gonna make *you* Number Four. Or hey, you know what?" He grinned, his eyes burning. "Hell, I just might kill you myself, you lying piece of crap. Right here. And then I'll be sure to put you on *his* tab."

It was one of those moments: when you don't know where you are or how you came to be there, but you understand with chilling clarity that nothing will ever be the same if you survive.

Johnny Lee drew his gun from its holster and pointed it at my face, the nose only a blur inches in front of my eyes.

"No, you son of a bitch." If such a thing is possible, his grin grew wider. "I'm not gonna kill you. Not this time. But that sure ain't gonna keep me from doin' the fun part." Johnny Lee pressed the gun against the bridge of my nose, hard, drawing even more blood, blinding me with the pain.

"You have the right to remain silent," he said.

"AND THEN THE SPIRIT OF my brother says to me -"

I wasn't really listening as Jud went on about his field-harvest at the bison ranch just hours earlier. The hulking Indian's tireless monologue about the spiritual lives of dead animals and dead ancestors was far less charming when heard through the bars of the Presidio County Jail.

Everyone, I imagine, wonders what it might be like to spend a night in jail. I'm not saying you wish you could. Just that you wonder what it might be like. And if you're anything like my age, your only experience behind bars is probably watching reruns of *The Andy Griffith Show*—you know, where the loveable town drunk named Otis lets himself into the cell to sleep it off and then lets himself out the next morning.

That jail in Mayberry is approximately nothing like the complex maintained by the upstanding citizens of Presidio County. And the people you meet on the inside are nothing at all like Otis.

For some reason, it took several hours to get me booked, my fingerprints taken, my wallet, cell phone and all-important set of restaurant keys signed for and taken from me. I was led back into the cell area, then placed in a single, large, concrete pen with two other lucky guys.

On the floor in the corner sat one unshaved Mexican with a knife slash across his nose. Sitting in a widening pool of urine, the Mexican kept mumbling what sounded like Hail Marys. But if my own teaching by the good sisters taught me anything, he was getting pieces of that prayer confused with the Our Father.

"Deliver us from evil," he kept saying, over and over. And I know that line isn't in the Hail Mary.

My other cellmate was vintage American redneck, a dying breed in my part of the world as the skin color year after year turns darker and the lingo spins more and more toward Spanish. The guy was wearing a ball cap from some minor-league team I didn't recognize and, to my surprise and discomfort, confused me immediately with somebody who gave one shit about him.

"I know, man," he said, grinning and showing off an ability to point his eyes in slightly opposite directions. "I know who put you in here."

I wasn't in a conversing mood, taking up instead a place against the wall and lowering myself into a pathetic, unbecoming squat. There were no chairs in this cell, no beds, no toilets. No *nothing*.

"Man, I know how ya feel," said my new best friend in the cap. "It's always a woman that does it, huh? Always! Who do you think knocked out ma front teeth?"

I hadn't looked closely at him up till then, but now he insisted upon it. He gave me a huge grin that revealed that two teeth on the top and one on the bottom were indeed missing, front and center. He kept on grinning, nodding at me in some apparent plea for understanding.

"Yep," he said. "And you know how she done it?"

"Nope."

This part seemed to delight him the most. "Shovel."

I tried to wave the guy to silence without seeming un-neighborly, which would be yet another mortal sin here in West Texas. But I also stared at my hands and started checking my wounds from the one-sided brawl with Johnny Lee, hoping the vibe of seriousness I gave off would shunt him away quickly. No such luck.

"Look at you, man," he said. "You done got the shit beat outta ya. I can tell you having woman trouble too."

"No. Really. I'm not."

"Aw hell, you don't have to be ashamed of it. I can tell you are. Every guy is, the first time she beats the shit outta you. Or the first time she has ya throwed in jail. But you know what the thing is, really?"

"No. What's the thing?" Led, I say, like a moth to the flame.

"The thing is this—wow, now, hold on. We ain't even met yet." He stretched out the gnarled, hairy hand that extruded from his red-and-black flannel work shirt. "My name's Billy Crabb Duncan. What's yours?"

"Brett," I said. "Baldwin."

"Sure, Brett. Pleased to meet ya. You do meet some mighty fine folks in here." He glanced around the cell. "If ya know what I mean."

"I'll bet."

"Well, Brett, the thing is, and you just gotta trust me on this, okay? I'm the goddamn poster child for what I'm about to tell you. The way it works is: Once they know they can put you in here—them women, I mean—once they figure that out, you never get to sleep good again. They're always pickin' a fight over some little bullshit thing, just so you'll wallop 'em. I mean, wallop 'em even a little bit. Nothin' real bad. And then there's always some deputy at your door, knockin' and shoutin' your damn name. You know what I'm sayin', Brett?"

"I guess," I said, looking at Billy Crabb Duncan for what I truly hoped would be the last time. "It's always the women that do it to you."

"Damn straight," concluded Billy Crabb.

Do you have any idea how long a night really is? If not, you need to spend one—and one will probably be enough—in the Presidio County Jail. I took off my overshirt and rolled it up to form a pillow, then stretched out on the concrete floor.

It was getting late, I knew: my restaurant was finishing a long but hopefully profitable night, and I had sneaked in one post-arrest cell phone call to Gilberto in my kitchen, giving him the one-sentence news update. Happily, I suppose, he was entirely unflustered by one of his number being locked up. It happened every day, he would have told me, had we had more than two seconds. It just didn't typically happen to me.

I slept like a baby all night on that concrete floor of the holding cell—in what I'm pretty sure were 10-to-20 second installments.

Like some law-enforcement rendition of a phone tree, Gilberto called Jud Garcia out at the bison ranch, and Jud called my attorney, Diane Cordova, who promised to make the trek down from her office in Fort Davis first thing in the morning. I have no idea who *Diane* called, but I hoped it was somebody who pulled a lot of strings around here. I'm certain Billy Crabb Duncan wasn't that guy.

So that's how I ended up sitting on the floor inside the bars, listening to Jud go on about the spirits of his animals and his ancestors. Diane called Jud to tell him she was on her way. It was about 9:30, though it felt hours later than that, when she finally walked in.

Diane, her blonde hair cut impossibly short and her contoured business suit a burnt orange affair that stopped a couple inches above the knee, glanced at the guard who'd escorted her in. The guard nodded his permission and left. She reached her right hand through the bars and let it rest lightly on my shoulder.

"You know," Diane said, "you seriously look like shit."

"I'm sorry."

Ever since we'd met as undergrads at Rice in Houston, laying eyes on Diane Cordova has made me want to shave extra close and recomb my hair. Of course, since we had a brief but intense history between us, she'd done more than most to mess my hair up in the first place.

I wanted that history back again, right now if possible. I knew, however, that Diane's four small children and one large husband made such a development unlikely.

"It's good you're beat up," she said.

"Huh?"

"It's one of the best things we've got on our side right now."

"Always glad to be of service."

"Yes, I do recall something like that about you."

I smiled.

"So," she said, "do we have to stop meeting like this?"

"Or next time, I'll have to bring you a rose."

This was certainly our all-time favorite story: how I'd given her a rose in the nocturnal shadows outside her dorm something like 20 years ago and then, in our enthusiasm for each other, we'd let the rose fall between our bodies and kind of, well, get ripped into perfumed pieces.

"Only do that," she said with a smile, "if we plan on making out."

I glanced awkwardly over at Jud, who was about as tall sitting down as Diane was standing up.

"You can't see it on my red skin," he said. "But I'm blushing right now."

"Wow, Diane." I turned back to her. "Law school made you even cooler than you were in college."

She sighed. "You really don't know the half of it."

After a few more moments, she displaced Jud in the metal folding chair outside the bars and had me tell her everything from the moment Meridyth Morgan walked into Mesquite, stopping me often to play 20 Questions. I love that about lawyers: they always want the hard, cold facts, and they never ask you what you're thinking or how you feel about it. Kept precisely in that mode, Diane would have been the perfect woman for me.

"Okay," she said, with a certain finality that delighted me. "Let me start gettin' you out of this goddamn place."

Diane returned with the same deputy half an hour later, and he proceeded to unlock the door. I glanced over at my fellow inmates, but both were curled up asleep in opposite corners, like battered boxers with way too many rounds left to go.

"That's it?" I asked, letting my most irresistible smile begin to form.

"Not quite," she said.

With Diane matching me step for step but Jud ordered outside to wait, we followed the deputy into what looked like every interrogation room I'd ever seen in the movies. Diane took the chair next to me on one side of a rickety metal table. The deputy made a move to put cuffs on me, but Diane blocked them with one immovable hand and a seductive almost-wink.

"Now deputy," she said, "I really don't think that will be necessary."

"But Johnny Lee—I mean, the sheriff told me —"

"You may give the sheriff my professional and, um, *personal* assurance my client will give him no trouble."

That was when Johnny Lee banged open the door, saw me without cuffs, glared with exasperation at his deputy, then followed the man's gaze downward to Diane.

"All right," the sheriff breathed out. "All hell is breaking loose in my county, and I can't even get help around here that'll keep cuffs on a suspect. But, okay, you'll see I don't have to be an asshole about this, Ms. Cordova."

"It would be most appropriate if you aren't one," she said. "In light of my client's numerous serious injuries. Of which I have now taken and transmitted digital photographs."

"You did *not.*"

"That's for you to find out." She smiled, and I was amazed how sexy she was playing the tough guy. Perhaps I'd liked this about her, without knowing it, all along. "But I would suggest you keep up with current technology a little better, Sheriff Crow."

"So, Ms. Cordova," Johnny Lee focused, settling into the lone folding chair across from us and pushing it back for extra legroom. "What I have here is a guy, your client, who has repeatedly attempted to impersonate an officer of the law, who has repeatedly hindered an ongoing homicide investigation—"

"I'm sure you understand, Sheriff, that those are merely allegations of a highly unspecific nature—nearly all of them, I'd wager, based on hearsay."

"Shit, lady, cut me some slack here. That's what I'm working with, is all. Every time I turn around, there's a new dead body. And joy of joys, every dead body seems to have had *this guy* as the last face they saw. What do you suggest I do about that?"

"Um, let me think." Diane made a little show of doing so, then brightened at finding the answer. "Maybe, like, your job?"

"Sure. Fine. But you people think it's so easy, right?"

"Hardly, sheriff."

"I had probable cause to take your client into custody and book him as a material witness. Hell, it was pretty much for his own good, knowing his special talent for stirrin' up shit in this town."

Diane motioned toward the large purple-blood welts on my face, then moved on to the deep scratches and slices on my neck and arms. "For his own *good*, you say?"

"Resisting arrest," said Johnny Lee. It was all he could do *not* to put a question mark at the end.

Diane let the silence that followed hang there in the room with us, allowing Johnny Lee to ponder just how many long miles he'd have to travel to make that one stick in any court of law. And, I felt her ask him without speaking a word, to achieve *what?* To get *where* in your homicide investigation, exactly?

"Aw screw it," he said at last. "You know what? I got me a national shitstorm right outside this jail. I got media from New York and all over Texas waiting to hear from me, along with guys from the FBI and the DEA, and probably the DAR and the ASPCA while they're at it."

"Comes with the badge, Sheriff Crow."

"Yeah," he said, with more sadness than I expected or understood until later. "It sure as hell does."

Johnny Lee stood abruptly, made a rough but unmistakable jerking gesture to the deputy and trudged out through the door. Diane smiled at me and gave me a bit of the same wink she'd just been using on every male in county government. It seemed only fair, considering our past.

"We're done here," she said.

As a kind of coda to the whole business, a confirmation from on high, by the time we'd hooked up with Jud at the front desk and I'd been handed a glorified sandwich bag filled with all the stuff I needed to live, Sheriff Johnny Lee Crow was indeed outside on the jailhouse steps.

Wearing his well-pressed Presidio County best beneath an immaculate white Stetson, he was speaking into a cluster of TV microphones while flanked by four guys in dark suits with American flag lapel pins.

I was about to ask Diane to take me away from all this, meaning the words but also enjoying the sexual fantasy, when my cell phone went off in my pocket. I realized, in that moment, that I'd never called the number I'd been left with Enrique's name scribbled on it, and perhaps it was him trying me again. But no.

"Brett Baldwin?" This was a question as I stepped away from Diane and Jud, a question delivered in a high-pitched and breathy male voice. "Am I speaking with the chef, Brett Baldwin?"

"Yes, sir, you are. May I help you?"

You can be a true jackass on your own time, but once you've been trained in the hospitality industry, you always offer to help everybody. The jackass, of course, can take over the conversation later.

"This is Mr. Gaylord Talley calling from Los Angeles," the voice said.

"You don't know me."

"No sir, I sure don't."

"I am the chief attorney for and indeed the largest stockholder in Constellation Films."

"Yes?"

"Which, you may know, owns the rights to Meridyth Morgan's next three motion-picture projects."

"I see." I didn't, as usual.

"And I have received a very strange anonymous phone call from somewhere down there, mentioning your name. And saying there's been some kind of trouble."

"Look, Mr. Talley. My caller ID says you're calling from California. Is that correct?"

"Actually," he almost seemed to giggle. "Not entirely."

"Well?"

"This would be my cell phone, of course," Mr. Gaylord Talley of Los Angeles said. "In point of fact, I'm calling you now from my suite at the Paisano Hotel, right here in Marfa. You and I most assuredly need to talk."

"HOW APPROPRIATE IT IS that I am staying here," Gaylord Talley said the next day as Jud and I let ourselves into his suite (as instructed) through its ornate double doors. "And Brett Baldwin would be you," he said, eyeing us both and settling on me, "I suppose."

"It would, sir."

"Do you know why this hotel is so appropriate for my stay?" Talley looked to be in his early 60s. "Or are you like the rest of your generation, so fixated on your own trivial wants and needs that you possess no sense of posterity."

"I'm not sure what you're getting at, Mr. Talley."

Jud said nothing. That was, after all, one of his specialties.

As he stood with a glass of something golden in his hand at the suite's sunny picture window, Gaylord Talley was dressed impeccably in a cream-colored silk suit that caressed every corner of his almost-tall frame with the attention of a tailor or a lover—whichever, as I like to say, comes first. His shirt was light blue and his tie a tad darker, with a pattern so delicate I couldn't exactly see it from where we stood in the entranceway.

Talley seemed young enough, I suppose, or at least his deep, rich suntan did. But his off-white hair was thinning significantly, slicked back from his tanned forehead in a manner most guys remember from their fathers.

"Do you have a clue about the landmark movie *Giant,* Brett? If I may be so familiar as to call you Brett?"

"Sure, everybody knows it was filmed around here."

"In 1956, to be precise. Based on the Edna Ferber novel, it was indeed filmed around here, as you put it with dazzling imprecision. And the stars of that film—Elizabeth Taylor, Rock Hudson, the doomed and gorgeous young James Dean, Hollywood legends all—well, Mr. Baldwin, they stayed at this very hotel throughout the filming. Possibly one of them in this very suite, though no one today can be trusted to tell the truth about that."

"That's cool."

"Yes, it is. Hardly my phrase, but my sentiment, exactly." Talley cleared his throat, then smiled as warmly as he could. "May I offer you a tequila, Mr. Baldwin? Your large friend is welcome to enjoy one as well."

"Going native, I guess? It just happens faster all the time."

Talley giggled, as he had more than once on the telephone. "No, sir. I know about you Texans and your national drink, the abysmal, ill-advised margarita. This is El Tesoro. It's the *anejo anniversio,* in fact, aged to perfection in white oak barrels that at one time brimmed with bourbon whiskey. My goodness, I might as well be an advertisement!"

"No thank you," I said. "For the drink, I mean. If you don't mind, I'd prefer to learn why you asked us to meet with you."

"Asked *you,* Mr. Baldwin." There was a darkness he could weave into his voice, I realized, that made it sound lower, like a black cloud crossing the afternoon sun. He was a lawyer in Hollywood, after all. He probably had to push a lot of people around. "With no intention of being rude, I did not in any way, shape or form invite you to bring a friend."

"You know the drill: he stays or I go."

"Oh Brett, Brett, Brett." I'm not sure I'd ever heard my name three times in a row before. Certainly never from a man. "Sometimes one feels so grand about making movies. And then other times, you hear the best movie lines come back at you, and you wish you'd just spent your life selling homeowners insurance."

Talley waved us both into chairs with his glass, refilled it from the bottle and turned his smile on Jud. "And by the way, what name might I use to call you?"

"This is Jud Garcia," I answered quickly.

"And a more impressive specimen I've seldom seen, I must say." Talley moved closer to Jud, edging around the coffeetable. "Might I perhaps talk you into returning with me to Los Angeles? I'm sure there are many in my circle who'd envy me having you. Quite the catch, I'd have to say."

"Ugh," said Jud.

"That's Injun talk," I explained helpfully. "For hell no."

"Such a shame." He looked at me, measuring me quickly and finding me wanting. "Such a waste."

There was nothing Jud or I could say to that.

So we waited, watching Talley sip the *anejo,* directing its smooth-sweet-smoky flavor notes to different sections of his tongue as though it were a Louis XIII cognac. He gracefully took up residence on the love seat across from us and set down his empty glass.

"So now, gentlemen," Talley said, threading his fingers together in front of his chest, "if that pathetic human need for banter has been satisfied, I say we should get down to serious business."

"I should say," said Jud, surprising me. I gave him my most fearsome corrective glare, which aimed at Jud Garcia was a total joke.

Then we both gazed at Talley, intently.

"As you may be aware, or should be able to surmise, when you contract to produce a major motion picture, there are many things of innate value involved. And as you would with your home or your car, or perhaps an important piece of heirloom jewelry, you would be well-served to purchase insurance to protect those valuable things."

"Like perhaps, your leading lady," I said.

Talley smiled in Jud's direction. "I'd say your friend is catching on, wouldn't you?"

"He catches on real good," Jud said.

"So, first, I am here after reaching some broad agreements with our firm's insurance company—even though, officially or henceforth, they have no idea that I'm here. No sirs, they do not."

"Henceforth," I said, profoundly.

"As for that anonymous phone call I told you that I received, I was not being quite totally honest with you."

"*Quel surprise*," offered Jud.

"*Ah, tu parle francais?*"

"Who, me?"

"No, of course you don't. That phone call was not anonymous. It came directly to my desk from Meridyth Morgan herself. The number had been blocked and did not hint at the call's geographic origin, but I have known Ms. Morgan for several years. And it was indeed she."

"It was her?" asked Jud.

"She," I reassured.

"To cut to the quick, gentlemen, Ms. Morgan's kidnappers are demanding a ransom for her safe return. Yes, I know. I've made plenty of movies. It's what kidnappers always do. They threaten to kill her if we do not file a claim with our insurance company immediately and pay them the maximum coverage amount, which would be $15 million."

"You tell them that?" I asked.

"No, somehow they already knew." Talley cleared his throat and dutifully pressed ahead. "So, our company can pay the kidnappers, who may or may not include her brother Enrique, $15 million from our policy and hope for her safe return to the picture. The picture," he stopped to giggle, "in more ways than one. That would be an option."

"You know, Mr. Talley. I'm a chef and Jud raises bison. You really need to be telling these things to the police."

"As time goes by—lovely song, that, and you can thank the movies—and as your knowledge deepens, Brett, you will realize the police are the *last* people on earth with whom I should be speaking."

"Okay." With one eye black-purple and a burning pain deep in my ribs, I couldn't think of much reason to disagree. "So that's, how'd you put it, one option."

"Another option, just something to consider, mind you, is contracting with someone independently who knows the people and knows this area, someone who might be able to get Meridyth—to re-kidnap her, if you like—and bring her back to us. I will be blunt, Brett and Jud, we would expect to achieve substantial savings if we were to pursue this particular, somewhat *sotto voce* plan. The good guys, as we might be tempted to call them, would never charge us as much as the bad guys, now would they?"

"*That* is the question," said Jud, speaking on behalf of the entire hamlet.

"And quite frankly, our people have made some delicate inquiries about you, Brett—and yes, about your native American friend as well. And we think you might be just the people to handle this for us. No one, however, told me precisely how large your friend would be."

"That would be a first," I said.

"I'll be happy," said Jud, "to provide a list of personal references from lady friends later."

"You may dislike him now," I added. "But you'll really hate him when you get to know him."

"This plan we're proposing to you has many advantages. It sidesteps the law enforcement establishment, which may or may not prioritize things quite the way we might wish. It saves all involved a great deal of money. And it makes use of talents who may leave no footprints, whose many tools…" He glanced at Jud. "… would probably involve less than perfect licensing and record keeping."

"Ah," I said.

"Ah," Jud added, to make the point.

"And of course, as always in these matters, we have no time to lose."

"I have just one question for you, Mr. Talley," Jud said. He rose from his seat, and that comes out to be a lot of rising. "You speak so lovingly, so almost orgasmically of saving a great deal of money. It has to make me wonder a little what you might be thinking about paying us."

"Of course, this *is* surely something I've never done before."

"Surely," Jud agreed.

"But it seems you'd have such low overhead, as it were, that you would simply help us for whatever we agreed seemed fair."

Jud looked at me. I was shocked. I thought I'd seen every version of Jud there was over the years, but this was not exactly any of those versions. It was as though the life behind his eyes had drained out, leaving only something cold and more deadly than dead, something that could not be stopped.

"Mr. Talley," Jud said, "may I trust you didn't travel all the way from Los Angeles to insult my friend and me?"

"But, I, uh —"

"And since you wouldn't think of doing such a thing, I'll put it to you this way." Jud moved to a place towering over Talley's mini-sofa, looking down upon him like God painted on a church ceiling—and not your basic smiling God either. "The kidnappers want $15 million for the safe return of Meridyth Morgan. We'll take on your little project for $4 million, a quarter of that upfront, before we lift a finger."

"Now, I must —"

"You must *nothing*," Jud rumbled, scaring even me a little. "Yes or no, right here and now. $4 million, with $1 million upfront. And non-refundable."

"I warned you," I tossed at Talley in the first available silence. "I was sure you'd hate him when you really get to know him."

THE SAME AFTERNOON WE made our deal with Gaylord Talley, or whatever you call what Jud and I finally toasted in his suite at the Hotel Paisano with glasses of El Tesoro *anejo,* I called Enrique Morgan on the number he'd left me. And I got him on the first hop.

"You're a chef, right?" he asked.

"Yes."

"Then what's the deal? You chefs don't return phone calls or what?"

"I'm sorry."

"It's probably too late now. We had to go at this a different way."

"Go at what?" I asked him, sitting at the cluttered desk in my office at the restaurant. For Jud and me to have half a prayer of succeeding, I had to get as much information out of Enrique as I could. And I had to do it without making him wonder why I was trying so hard. "What are you talking about? And where the hell is Meridyth?"

"Meridyth is here, with me."

"Is she okay?"

"Oh, so you *do* care. When you didn't call me back, we both figured you weren't interested."

"I care, Enrique." I struggled to keep my breathing even. "Look, I don't know your sister that well. But she came to ask my help. And she seems like a good person, who certainly is trying to do the right thing for you. And we knew each other in high school. You need to appreciate that. And you need to help me get her out of all this safe. Really."

"I want her safe too."

"Enrique, where are you?"

"Ha ha," he snorted into the phone. "That's a good one. Why do you think this is an untraceable cell phone, eh? I tell you where we are, and I wonder who'll get here first: the FBI, the DEA and your good buddy the sheriff."

"He's no good buddy of mine."

"I suspect you'll end up being damn grateful for that."

Enrique was speaking in nervous scattershots, his voice moving forward in spurts until awkward stops, and for a moment I wondered if he used drugs every bit as much as he sold them. I also thought of things I'd read about crazed serial killers, about the way they started slow and deliberate but ended up falling apart, their personalities unraveling, killing on the slightest frenzied impulse.

I had no idea if that's what we were dealing with here. For Meridyth's sake—hell, for *our* sake—I certainly hoped not.

"No sir," he laughed again. "That I'm not gonna tell you. At least until it can do us some good. And like I said, we're working directly now."

"The movie company?"

"Yeah, that was the whole idea. We just thought you could be a go-between. Maybe we just don't need you anymore, huh?"

"Listen, Enrique. You need me as the go-between." I was improvising, and I had never been much good at improvising. "Everybody with a gun is out there looking for you. You could stand to have somebody like me involved. You know, between them and you. Who can bring you the money and not try to arrest you for a big, fat reward."

"Arrest me?" He laughed. "Nobody wants to arrest me, Brett. That ain't gonna happen. What they want to do is *kill* me."

"To shut you up? Like Meridyth told me?"

"Yeah, that about covers it."

"Is she okay? Please tell me that. She looked in pretty bad shape at the hospital." There was a feeling at the edge of my mind, and before I could think about it, I just said it. "And I, uh, I need her to be okay."

"Meridyth's fine. We brought that doctor, you know. And all her IVs and medications."

"Her doctor's there?"

"Listen, Brett. If this thing works right and we get the money, Meridyth and Dr. Bambawhatever will be totally free to go. Safe and sound. It's that easy."

"Easy," I repeated. It was so damn easy I had no idea how Jud and I were ever going to pull it off.

"So, Enrique, this is all about the money?"

"Damn right it is. Great big freakin' piles of money. What we plan to do with it is, well, that's my business. The only thing you can do is help me get it. Or not."

"I want to help."

"Why?"

Part of me was afraid he'd ask that question. Fact is, I'd been asking it myself. The chance to split $4 million with Jud figured in, for sure—though the odds of anything resembling success seemed so remote that I hadn't given the money a single thought. No, I realized, for me it wasn't about the money.

At this moment, I understood that it was and always would be about Meridyth. Sure, Meridyth as she was now, a lovely and iconic star on some big screen somewhere. But also Meridyth as she crumbled into that stupor of alcohol and regret at my restaurant. And most of all, it was about Meridyth as she used to be, at age 14, smiling at me under those stadium lights, kickstarting and then breaking my heart with a note pressed into my hand in the icy winter darkness.

I had deserted her back then, through no fault of my own. I wasn't going to desert her again. And I had to find her, to rescue her, so I could tell her so.

"Enrique, listen to me," I said. "I need you to put Meridyth on the phone. Now."

There was movement of the cell phone, muffled voices, a snap of something hitting something else, followed by a long, drawn-out rise from static to clarity as the receiver refound its signal.

"Brett?" Meridyth's voice quivered, and for once in my life I had no fear at all that she was only acting. "Oh my dearest Brett. Are you really riding to my rescue?"

"This time, apparently, yes."

"Oh honey, I just knew you would."

"Then I wish you'd done a better job of letting me in on the secret."

"I tried. You can't say I didn't try."

"No, I can't. But next time, don't be so subtle, okay? I'm a chef. I don't do subtle."

"Deal."

I held the phone tight against my ear, my cheek, listening to her voice from somewhere that sounded very far away. She sounded small, but then again, weren't we all in some way? Except Jud, of course—Jud, who held, who *was,* the key to so many deceptions that would carry me to Meridyth and some new life I'd wanted without knowing it.

"But Brett," she said, almost feverishly, "you have to listen to me now, okay, darling? This is so important."

"I'm listening."

"It's good and necessary that you bring the money. Enrique needs the money, and all he wants is to finally do some good in his life. He has done so much that wasn't good. Do you understand?"

"Yes," I said, having no clue.

"But what matters is that no one hurts him, Brett—it's all that matters to me. You know that, yes? You know that nothing will be worth anything if they come here and find him, if they kill him?"

"I understand. That's why I'm the one bringing the money."

That wasn't entirely a lie.

After Meridyth and I said our crazy-silly-passionate goodbyes, I had her put Enrique back on. Somehow, I had to close this deal. And this deal was with him, not with Meridyth.

"Listen, man, we really can do this," I told him. "Since you're already in touch with the film company, you can just tell them I'll be their delivery man. Insist on it. They give the $15 million to me and I bring it straight to you. Trust me on this, okay?"

"Jesus, when you've been on the inside any time at all, you never trust anybody again."

"You can trust me. Ask Meridyth."

The silence meant he was thinking about it, running his whole plan, changes and all, through this latest of opportunities, this latest of dangers. Yet, as I knew he was thinking, he *was* drawing closer to his goal, to his dream, and I was sounding more and more like the guy who could make it happen. Hadn't I been part of their idea for this from the start?

"Now listen, Enrique. You've really got to tell me where you all are. I mean, no funny business. I need to start planning this thing, and every place you might be, well, makes it different. That's all. I'm not," I promised in my best honest salesman voice, "going to ever show up on your doorstep without $15 million."

"I don't know."

"Are you in Mexico, man? Across the border? That might be a real mess, you know. Everybody thinks you're in Mexico, hiding out with Victor Morales."

"Hell no." Again, that bitter, exhausted laugh, coming from behind the prison bars that remain always, even after the physical prison bars are taken away. "Not with Morales. And not in Mexico. We're in this tiny weird-ass town in Texas that isn't even a town at all. Come on, Brett. You know *Terlingua,* don't you?"

THINK PRIEST PERFORMING A BELOVED SACRAMENT. Think chef clarifying a beloved stock. And then you might have some idea what it's like watching and listening to Jud as he prepares his beloved ammo beneath a low-hanging lamp at his reloading table in what used to be my parents' living room.

"Look at this," he said, pressing one open hand in my direction and using a finger from the other one to roll a small silver projectile around his palm.

"I *am* looking. It's a bullet, right?"

Truth be known, I was more drinking a cold Shiner than looking at anything as the afternoon desert sunlight poured in through dust floating in waves that would have done an ocean proud. Housekeeping wasn't Jud's strong suit—or mine either, for that matter—except when it meant keeping dirt and grime away from his weaponry, which had the good fortune to be sealed in tall wood-and-glass cases that covered every wall of the room.

At least it was afternoon, I reassured myself. The last time I drank beer while Jud did something else (our two most recurring job descriptions), it was something like ten in the morning. I was getting better.

I'd hitched a ride with Paco the dishwasher out to the Marfa Lights Viewing Area to reclaim my Jeep Cherokee, which seemed none the worse for my night enjoying the county's hospitality. I'd headed out to Jud's immediately to fill him in on my conversation with Enrique.

We *needed* to talk about that. But really, can you chat about Saturday's Texas Tech game with a brain surgeon handling a life-or-death incision? You'd better not try it with Jud when he's busy reloading.

"Goes in small and very clean," he explained. "Into the skull, preferably."

"Good place to aim for," I said.

"Better place to hit."

Turning the silver bullet in the light, Jud showed me that it was hollow.

"By the time it bangs around into bones and stuff, it's all torn up. So when it comes out the back of the skull, well, you really don't want to be there."

"I don't want to be there already."

"Very effective," he said, then considered. "If that's what you're looking for."

"That may very well be what we're looking for."

He set the hollowpoint upright like a tiny nuclear warhead on the table, where something like a dozen different types of gunpowder were mounded like spices you see in a Turkish market. They weren't as colorful as spices, being gunpowder, but no two types were exactly the same shade of gray-black, or operated exactly the same way when ignited inside a gun. That had been the first lecture of the day, which used up 39 minutes and my whole first beer. You can count yourself lucky you missed that one.

"So," Jud said, and no matter what else happened, it was always a bit of a shock when Jud caught a subject in his crosshairs, "Enrique is holding Meridyth in Terlingua."

"That's what he says."

"When are we going after her—I mean, meeting with him?"

"Don't know yet. We have to go back to Talley this afternoon, remember? He's gonna get the money sent here—for us, not for Enrique—and when we know he's got it, then we head for Terlingua, I guess."

"Spicy," Jud said.

"Huh?"

"It's the chili place, Terlingua. Where they've been having that damn chili cook-off for like a thousand years. Two of them, in fact. Kinda like a battle of the bands, a cook-off of cook-offs. I was on a chili team there once, you know."

Jud never ceased to catch me off guard. "What, did they need somebody to go shoot all the meat?"

"Nah, just helpin' out. We drank a lot, if I recall."

"That was back when you still drank?"

"If I recall."

I had never set foot in Terlingua, though it certainly carried deep mythological weight among professional Texans, of which there are more than a few. I'd been to Big Bend National Park, which wasn't far off. And I'd been flown in by private jet years ago to help the mildly bizarre Lajitas Resort with one of its regular restaurant makeovers—new menu and all that—flashing over brown dirt and cactus to suddenly swoop in for a landing amid the blindingly green, bankruptingly watered golf course.

But no, I carried no Terlingua stamp on my passport. And I had the nerve to call myself a Texan!

"Kinda cool place," Jud said. "If you like living in your truck."

I related to Jud, with the same kind of factual concentration I always tried to use with Diane Cordova, minus the flirting of course, all elements of Enrique's responses that seemed to matter.

They were in Terlingua. Meridyth had that Indian doctor with her, and we were supposed to rescue him too, though nobody was giving us a dime for that. And just the overall sequence ahead of us: Make an appointment to deliver the ransom money, grab Meridyth and hopefully her doctor, and then shoot our way out.

"Hmm," Jud said considerately, "you okay with the shooting-our-way-out part?"

"I guess."

"No, I don't mean saying it." He looked at me intently, his black eyes almost glowing within the frame of his deeply lined red face. "I mean *doing* it."

"Well, really, I suppose I figured one of us had to do the talking, and then the other of us had to do the shooting."

"Hmm, something tells me I won't be saying much."

We agreed it could be done, as always with a little luck and a favorable location. Enrique would pick the location, as people in his position always did, so any plan we made couldn't be about the set-up. It had to be about us, what we said and did, and what weapons we carried with us without tipping anybody off.

And when any or all of that let us down, there was always the four-million bucks. That and the lovely woman waiting for me would be motivation enough. What I couldn't measure precisely was how much this motivation would matter when Jud's hollowpoints and many more of the lethal wonders he'd shown me over the years started howling in the direction of my depressingly pierceable hide.

We caught up with Talley a couple hours later having dinner in Jett's Grill, the restaurant in the Hotel Paisano named after James Dean's character in *Giant*. Talley was so much a creature of Hollywood and its carefully tended myths that he couldn't get enough of this stuff.

"Gentlemen," he said, rising from his seat to show off a different variation on cream-colored silk suit with a different variation on color-coded shirt and tie. "Perhaps you'd care to join me for a bite? I seldom dine alone in Los Angeles, and it's beginning to depress me a little here in Marfa, truth be told."

"I know," I said. "I see it every night at my place. Lonely diners, I mean."

"Of course, there *are* compensations. This wonderful claret-like red wine, for instance."

"Claret," offered Jud, speaking as the ghost of bottles past. "What the Brits like to call red wine from Bordeaux. Since they never call anything by its real name. Seems an odd choice for dinner here in Texas."

"I would have thought so as well. But the wine is made right here in your charmingly backwoods state. Winery called Becker, I believe." He glanced around. "Though the waitstaff seems to have removed my bottle."

"Maybe," I said, "they think you've had too much to drive home."

"It's only an elevator, dear boy. Years of practice."

"And actually, Gaylord—if I may be so familiar as to call you Gaylord." He laughed, as I guessed he would. "We make a whole lot of wine here in Texas. More than any other state except New York, Oregon, Washington and, what's that other little place?"

"California?" Jud asked.

"Yeah, that place."

"It's mostly Chateau Bubba down here, I imagine."

"Used to be. Not anymore. Take your claret, for instance."

"Excellent suggestion," Talley said, lifting the glass. "I think I shall."

Once we'd sat down and filled him in on my chat with Enrique, passing on his invitation to dinner, we asked Talley to put our plan in motion. We had already deposited his first check for $1 million but were still waiting for the bank to say it had cleared. Based on my read, that wasn't likely to be a problem—though I've been surprised before.

More critical, though, was the rest of the money. We couldn't get at it until we returned with Meridyth, hopefully with all three of us breathing, but Jud insisted on a plan that would assure us it was really here.

"No check-in-the-mail kinda thing," he stipulated. I could only nod my assent.

"By the way," I asked, having no idea where this question came from, "how will the money be coming here? By pink-and-lavender armored car from West Hollywood?"

"Oh? Now that's funny, sir. I mean it. It's certainly a visual to which I can relate." He thought a moment. "Let's just say it won't be arriving at your local Western Union. You won't find me doing business at a place like that."

Oddly, I do business at a place "like that" all the time.

So many of my workers are sending all or huge chunks of their paychecks home to family members in Mexico, there's somebody almost every week who begs me to go and make the transfer for them. I know such things and places all too well. And judging by the fees my guys were paying for the likes of wiring $274.38, I didn't want to see the bill for sending our final $3 million.

"No, gentlemen," said Gaylord Talley, dabbing his lips with the napkin, looking around for his waiter and the rest of his Texas-made British claret-French Bordeaux wine. "It won't be coming that way at all."

EARLY THE FOLLOWING MORNING, especially by restaurant standards, Gilberto and I made the drive north to Fort Davis—no longer a cavalry fort, of course, built to protect us from the evil redskins who had the nerve to think this was their land. It was instead a reasonably attractive town in the mountains of the same name.

As we passed into the higher altitudes from our "low life" down in the desert, the sky seemed bluer, the air seemed fresher and small bits of green began to appear along the roadside. Living and working where Gilberto and I do, you kind of forget that green is a color found in nature.

We were meeting Diane Cordova in her office to finish my last will and testament.

"Gustavo called me this morning," Gilberto said, staring straight ahead at the two-lane climbing further into the mountains. "Uncle Gus?" He turned enough to see me nod. "He said he enjoyed meeting you. And he is sorry he had to leave so... so fast."

"He did race off a little bit, when the guys in the Sherman tank came to get him."

"Is precaution, you know. He must tenga much cuidado, jefe. The people he work for, they no very nice."

No very nice. Such an understatement.

And the fact that I was about to meet in person with these people, about to try to beat them at part of their own game, said it all about this trip to sign papers with my attorney.

Gilberto, so often a man of few words, wasn't finished.

"Gustavo he say he worried about you." Again, my sous chef looked for a reaction, just as he does when I'm tasting a sauce he's made for one of his nightly specials. "You know?" Unlike with a sauce, I wasn't sure what my reaction was supposed to be. "Jefe, he say. Victor Morales knew he met to you. That he ask about you."

"*Morales?* Is Gus okay?"

Gilberto laughed, looking down at the scarred and burn-discolored hands in his lap, then out his side window at the fast-changing terrain going from brown to green. "Yeah, Gus is okay. He tell Morales he tell you nothing."

"Which is true, more or less."

"Si, jefe. Morales know he tell you nothing. They have worked together for very, very long time. Gus has see what happen."

"Telling me nothing is good for business?"

"Very good for business, jefe."

Diane's two-room office suite was in an old red-brick building near the center of Fort Davis, one of those landmarks that somebody thought would be cool to renovate and fill with lawyers and CPAs to pay the mortgage. From the number of empty offices, I wasn't sure how the mortgage was being paid. But Diane, I'm sure, carried her share.

On the second floor, with a view of probably somebody else's second floor blocked by the leafy top of a tree, a cute, impossibly young secretary asked us to wait in two chairs by her desk while Diane finished up a conference call.

"It's about a deposition," the secretary filled in, unnecessarily. "She shouldn't be long."

She wasn't. But before we could even drag the pair of dark wooden chairs up to Diane's desk, she waved us to stop in our tracks. "Know what, guys? I'm starving. What is it now—breakfast, lunch?"

"In between, maybe."

"Good." Today her suit was dark blue. All her suits were the same cut, and as a fan I was just as glad. "And considering that you're two chefs who didn't bring me a damn thing to eat, I happen to know just the place."

The café one block over and another block down was packed. Clearly, this was where all those Stetson-topped lawyers and CPAs were officing these days, rather than leasing in Diane's building.

The coffee never ran out, for one thing. And it was better than any office coffee I've ever tasted, even in the corporate offices that ran dozens or hundreds of *restaurants*. Plus, as a café that specialized in "Mexican breakfast," this place—Amalia's, it was called—started serving early and kept serving late, with food you were destined to love no matter what time of day it was.

"So say it, guys. I'm a genius, yes?"

"There you go again, Diane," I said. "Leading the witnesses."

We got a pot of coffee and mugs for the table, then made quick work of ordering food. No matter what you ordered, it was all made with rice, refried beans, molten cheese and corn tortillas, with ladle after ladle of red-brown chile gravy. Only the question of eggs-or-no-eggs decided whether what you were eating was breakfast or not.

While we waited for our huge platters, and indeed even while we forklifted cheese-oozing mega-bites into our mouths, Diane kept up a steady barrage of questions and explanations. I'm not sure how she directed the gravy away from all the documents and sub-documents and addendums to the other addendums she had me sign that morning. And knowing my style of eating, I'm especially not sure how I managed to follow suit. Gilberto got off easy, having to sign only a handful of the long, carefully paragraphed sheets of words he didn't begin to understand.

"So," Diane said. That sentence didn't get very far, since she had to finish swallowing a bite of her migas, the scrambled eggs even more so with strips of fried tortillas and slices of jalapeno. And that required a wash-down with two gulps of black coffee. "So guys…"

"Did everything work out?"

"Essentially, yes. Excellent lawyering, I think it would be called here in Texas."

"Absolutely."

"So Brett, here's your part. Since you're just renting it, there's nothing that needs doing with your house in Marfa except to stop living in it."

"Which presumably comes with the territory. If I die."

"Exactly. And we've confirmed that your former residence in Houston—outside Houston, to be precise—belongs entirely to your ex-wife, per the divorce decree and settlement."

"Call her Julie. I hate that 'ex-wife' stuff."

"OK, Julie. Sheesh. Per your instructions over the phone on the 17th, I have treated your restaurant as your primary possession, your chief thing of value to leave to your heirs. And since you and Julie have no children from your marriage, I have divided the restaurant evenly between her and your mother, also domiciled in Houston. And since nobody in Houston in their right mind…"

"Other than me."

"Well, your honor, I rest my case. Anyway. Since you've spoken with Julie and your mother, and neither is interested in or able to assume the operation of Mesquite, that's where this second set of documents comes in."

"Like magic," I observed.

"Indeed."

Another stack of papers emerged from Diane's seemingly bottomless satchel. The satchel was a bit like her appetite for food, wine and, long before her marriage and children, me. I liked that about her, a lot. She turned to Gilberto.

"Now," she said, "are you sure you don't have a couple million bucks somewhere? To buy the place outright?"

As he and his people always do in this country and, sadly, perhaps forever will, Gilberto reacted with confusion and fear—a reflection, I understood (better than Diane, apparently), of the precariousness of their situation. But then Gilberto got the joke, made sure in Diane's eyes that it *had* been a joke, and then replied with a simple smile. His teeth, thankfully, were much better than his uncle's.

"Si, senora. I mean, no, I am sure I do not have two million bucks."

"Pity." Diane glanced at the first page. "So in that light, which is how I have approached this so far, I have here signatures from Julie and your mother, Brett, that essentially will sell your restaurant to Gilberto Cruz immediately upon settlement of your estate."

"Dying and selling," I couldn't resist the wordplay. "Capitalism at its finest."

"Yes. And as agreed on Page 7, you, Gilberto will pay a note on the restaurant each month, using a percentage of the revenues from the operation and with the restaurant as your collateral on what amounts to a loan. A mortgage, if you prefer. You will essentially be buying the restaurant on time."

"Just like," Gilberto chuckled, "everything else."

"It's the American dream, my friend," Diane said.

"The Mexican dream also," said Gilberto.

We took turns signing all the documents, which had been conveniently pre-marked with color-coded tabs wherever there was a need. In law, as in all things worth doing, Diane was very thorough.

"Now remember, G," I said, summarizing things between my last couple bites of red-gravied huevos rancheros. "This don't mean shit unless I die. So don't get any wild and crazy ideas."

I was clearly having enough of those for the both of us.

As seemed to befit my new life as a quasi-criminal, I started my glowing new relationship with Gilberto Cruz by lying to him. I told him I had to drop him at the restaurant as soon as we got back from Fort Davis, so I could go visit with a big catering client about a Christmas party in December.

"Good time for it," was all Gilberto said.

But, once he had vacated the passenger seat carrying his copies of all the documents, I raced home to check my email on the four-year-old mail-order Dell laptop I kept on my kitchen table. God knows, par for the course when you do what I do for a living, I certainly never ate any meals there.

The email from Gaylord Talley was waiting in my Gmail inbox. "See," was all it said, "absolutely no Western Union."

Following the instructions set down by Jud to the letter—Jud brought out the best in people that way—Talley had sent me two pdf files, one showing a receipt for the $3 million deposited locally, the other showing that same amount as the current balance. The account numbers had all been deleted from my version, of course. Far be it from Gaylord Talley to make life too easy for us.

"It's in," I told Jud over my cell phone. It was the only phone service I kept at my house.

"Then call Enrique and set it up. For tomorrow, I'm thinking. Though again, it's up to him. He's got her and we want her. And Brett, you need to *seem* a little put upon by all this. Remember, you're just somebody that got dragged in."

"What, Jud? Are you implying that I'm *not* put upon?"

We hung up, and I retrieved the crumpled note with number Enrique had left at my restaurant. As always, he was Enrique-on-the-spot.

"The insurance money?" he asked.

"Yeah. I met yesterday with the guy from the studio, as I told you I would. And he was the guy to file the claim on their business protection policy. And he was the guy to have the money transferred here, so I can bring it to you."

"So, tell me this. If he has all the money—this Gaylord Talley? That's who Meridyth told me would come. Is it him?"

This seemed to be going in a weird direction. But sometimes you just have to go in that weird direction with it.

"Yeah. That's the guy."

"So, if this Talley has all the money, why don't I just get it directly from him?"

Oh shit! Here we go again.

"Enrique, look." Jud had been right. "We've gone over this. I don't know you, and I barely know Meridyth. And I don't give much of a damn about any guy in a silk suit from Hollywood. See? Meridyth asked me to help, is all, and then she asked me, you know, to deliver the money. To keep everybody else away from you. Which seems like a pretty good trick these days. Come on, man. What the hell am I gettin' outta this? I'm just trying to help."

"Yeah?"

"But I sure as hell don't have to."

"Okay, okay. Take it easy, Brett, all right. I got you talkin' to me on the phone and I got Meridyth talkin' to me in the room here, like two inches away. And I gotta think, okay? That's all."

"So think, Enrique. I know you can do it. But think fast, cuz I'm pickin' up the money from Talley about -" I paused, giving my bald-faced Texas-size lie some credibility. "—20 minutes from right now."

"Well—"

"You thinkin' yet?"

"Geez, man. Okay. You're on. Tomorrow. I mean, let's get this done. I can't have you running around town with $15 million of my money in your pocket, now can I? It's a dangerous world out here."

"So I gather."

Over the next ten minutes, Enrique described the place we'd be making our big exchange. It was a site, that's all—an abandoned ranch three miles beyond Terlingua. I hadn't even known there *were* three miles beyond Terlingua.

Jud seemed pleased when I called him. He knew the area from years and chili cook-offs past, and might even have seen the ranch from a rough patch of some country highway. Then again, there were plenty of abandoned ranches in our part of West Texas, most of them not lucky enough to have movie stars bidding against dot-comers for that special pride of ownership.

"So you're on your way out here, right?" he asked.

"What do you mean? I have a restaurant to run."

"You might consider letting that damn place run itself for a change," Jud said, his voice flat, serious. "We're gazing across the battlefield now, at some real badass Injuns. You and me had better pick out some excellent artillery."

"NO BEER FOR YOU," JUD SAID.

"I know.

"This is serious."

"I said I *know.*"

We stood in the center of the living room in which I'd spent my early childhood, now covered with enough gun racks that, filled with broadswords instead, would have made a medieval warlord feel safe from the peasantry. I couldn't rule out the existence of broadswords in any building that passed for Jud's residence; I just couldn't see any in this room.

The cases were unlocked, every one of them, each key still in its lock. Some cases, in fact, had already poured forth handguns and boxes of shells onto folding tables that had appeared in my absence.

"Me first," said Jud. "I think that will impart the proper sobering attitude, even though in your case that's setting the bar awfully high."

"Come on. You're already not letting me drink."

"And besides," he said, studying me as though to determine my worth, "it may take some trial and error to find what's exactly right for you."

Jud Garcia, haberdasher from hell.

"OK, so listen and learn, cuz I'm not making this shit up." Jud turned to the nearest table and picked up a stocky, short-barreled black number that looked like it was borrowed from Dick Tracy. "This'll be my main handgun for this mission, and I'll carry it in a shoulder holster. It's called the M&P 340, and it's made by Smith & Wesson."

"I've heard of those two guys."

"I'll bet. It's small, it's light, and it packs a punch—it's a .357 magnum, in fact, which means it'll do whatever it needs to do. It fires five rounds—"

"Which won't be enough?"

"Which won't be enough. So, for that special, highly desirable place in my pants, here's what else I'm taking along." Jud set down the M&P 340 and picked up a sleeker, more modern-looking piece of work. "This is a Glock 20, which can handle a magazine with 33 rounds. There is a more compact model out there, the G19, but I like this one for its penetration."

"Am I old enough to hear this?"

"Yeah, especially if you want to get any older. This gun is basically proof that the police and military of about 100 countries have some idea what they're doing. When it comes to weapons anyway."

"That's enough, right? Five rounds plus 33? I mean, you can kill 38 people with those."

"I would certainly enjoy the experience. But the deal about being armed, Brett: the first thing people do is try to disarm you. You've got to be ready for that."

"Like, maybe judo?"

"Nah, I've found that a Centennial Airweight works much better." He lifted one of those from the table and held it out for my perusal. "It's a Smith & Wesson too, an ankle-carry revolver, and a lot of guys I know consider it an essential part of 'business casual.' Better than the so-called Baby Glocks, though *they* can be pretty good to have around too."

"I'm sure."

"And there's always the problem of sock lint."

"Hadn't heard about that problem, somehow."

"Well, it's a big one if it jams your damn gun. The Centennial has a mostly closed action, you see? No crevices, no sock lint."

"Martha Stewart would say that's a good thing."

"Yeah," Jud said, gathering the three handguns into a tight Indian powwow at the center of the table. "Like I said, I'm not just making this shit up."

"OK," I said. "What about me?"

"We're not finished with *me* yet."

"Jesus. Can you carry all this?"

Jud smiled. "Been workin' out."

He reached into the gun case and pulled out the strangest-looking device loosely resembling a weapon that I have ever seen. No part of its construction was included for looks, which makes it different from 99% of the guns you see in the typical Texas hunter's arsenal. It was all action pieces and hard edges, until you expanded your vision a bit and imagined it killing people.

"Remember the old M16, the M4?" Jud noted my blank expression, letting out a breath of extreme dismissal. "Well, if you'd ever bothered to serve our country proudly in some otherwise worthless piece of shit nowhere, you'd know one or both. They call this the Bushmaster Gas Piston Carbine. I just call it fighting fire with fire."

"How so?"

"You really don't keep up with the news, do you?"

"Not if I can help it."

"All those drug lords slaughtering each other along the border? Like in Nuevo Laredo? Brett, *this* is what they're using. And they get them mostly from your old stomping ground, Houston."

"It seemed such a friendly place at the time."

"The cartels pay anybody they can think of, Americans if possible but any reasonable facsimile, to go into gun shops and buy these guns. Just perfect for a little good-natured recreation, as you can see. And the shops keep selling them, even if the same guy comes in for 12 or 15 over just a few weeks. The feds are having a fit, but can't seem to stop the smuggling or even slow it down."

"Why the hell not?"

"Son, if you were a better American, you'd know that already." Jud grinned, putting his hand over his heart. "God bless that Second Amendment."

Finally, it was my turn. Though Jud hadn't revealed the details of his plan yet, it obviously involved me being unarmed. The first thing they'd do is check me for weapons, and the presence of anything more lethal than a bag of marbles would set off a chain reaction I didn't care to imagine.

Still, Jud had considerately picked out a gun for my use, a shotgun, he said, stepping over to another of his cabinets. It didn't look like any shotgun I'd ever seen, but I was beginning to expect that by now. The thing looked more like a pistol with its own extended grip, with an angled tube-like stock jutting out the back and a pair of top-and-bottom barrels poking out the front.

"And the stock includes swing swivel studs," Jud said.

"I just figured they were talkin' about us."

This was the Remington Model 870, Jud explained as he settled it lightly into my arms, a pump-action 12-guage of the type many hunters would use for duck, dove or quail. But this was the TAC, or tactical, edition, with bells and whistles added over time from use in law enforcement.

"I paid a lot for this sucker too, so you better not lose it." Jud's look darkened as a very unpleasant thought crossed his mind. "I've been assuming you've fired a shotgun before. Am I making that up?"

"Sure I have," I said proudly. "I used to go hunting with my father. We shot ducks in the marshes by Matagorda. So yeah, absolutely. I went hunting once."

"Once?"

"It was pretty funny too. It became a kind of family legend, such as our family had any. They say I almost sank the boat with spent shells to get my limit of five ducks."

Jud reached across the space between us, tightened both his hands around the Remington and yanked it away from me. He even started to put it back in the case but reconsidered, carrying it over a bit reluctantly to join the other guns on the table with piles of their appropriate ammunition.

"Hell, safe is the ultimate relative term," he said. "You're still more likely to help out by hitting something with a big spray of pellets than with one little bullet." He shook his head, staring at the floor. "Shit, I just hope it's not me."

As the hour grew late and the outside grew dark and still, Jud and I invited our wives to join us one last time on my family's former sleeping porch. And since we didn't *have* any wives, they didn't show up. So we talked about the plan, in as much detail as we could, with Jud drawing diagrams of things on several sheets of paper.

In solidarity with my beer-less state, or perhaps in hope of maintaining it, he refrained from smoking anything wonderful and illegal in his pipe.

"Is this," I asked, more than once, "much of a plan?"

"It's humble but our own."

"It seems less about how good the plan is than how good we are."

"Aren't they always," Jud said.

"Really, do you think this is enough of a plan?"

The vision of Jud Garcia channeling Oliver Hardy is not one you hope to see more than once in this lifetime, or for that matter, at all. But

I'd swear that's who he was channeling in that briefest of moments when he said, "I *certainly* hope so."

On the phone, Enrique had described the ranch house as being atop a mesa, constructed therefore along the modified knight-and-his-castle plan that came into vogue around 1273. Build high, the glossy magazines of that day would have instructed, and kill anybody you don't know who tries to climb up. There was a road up to the house, a kind of switchback, he'd said, plus a lot of small, rough trails that used to be used by Indians. Jud smiled at that part.

While drawing on his sheets of paper, Jud tried on a lot of phrases to describe how I'd be when I walked into the open. Alone. By myself. Without anybody else. Some of the phrases were more like letters, though, like S, O and L. But I would do all this, carrying a large case that was supposed to carry $15 million. Except that it wouldn't. That, you see, was how our plan was so brilliant.

There was an old, abandoned barn to the east of the old, abandoned house, which is generally how you know things go together in our part of the world. That and the absence of any other things for somewhere between two and a hundred-fifty miles. All of them, including Meridyth, would be gathered in the barn, Enrique said, where they had been staying, waiting for me and the money.

He probably didn't really mean *all* of them.

I would need to draw him out to talk, along with anybody working for him. They would surely be armed. And I would insist, before showing them any money, upon seeing that Meridyth was present and unharmed. Hopefully along with that Ay-rab doctor, as Johnny Lee Crow described the medical man from Mumbai or wherever.

Get as close to Meridyth and the doctor as I could, Jud instructed. They might need help. They might need protection. It would be my job to provide whatever they needed.

Jud, for his part, would do basically everything else. He would come at them fast and hard, using the element of surprise as much as he/we could maintain it. And like a magician in a traveling side show, he would count on their attention being elsewhere while he did what he needed to do, which probably would include killing all of them. This would require, Jud explained, a lot of diversions.

"Do we need to find an all-night diversion store?"

"Nah," Jud said. "Them I got."

It was only then, as happened so often out at the bison ranch with its on-again, off-again cell phone signal, that I felt mine vibrating in my pocket. And also as happened often, it showed the digital evidence of having vibrated in vain many times that night already.

"This is Brett Baldwin," I said, intuitively checking my watch and rolling my eyes. It was 11:47. Only then did I realize it was my own restaurant calling.

At first, all I heard was a series of deep, heaving breaths, and possibly a sigh or a liquid whimpering groan.

"Hello, may I help you?" I said, the way we always do in the darkness, insisting that all dangers reveal themselves instantly at our command. I was answered only by more loud, erratic, violent breathing.

Finally, "Se... se... senor?"

"Hello?" I thought I recognized the voice, though with all I now understood to be hysterical crying, I couldn't be sure. "Manuelita?"

"Si... Senor Brett."

"Manuelita, you need to tell me what's wrong." I remembered that her English was the worst in my kitchen, but in that terrible instant my years filled with kitchen Spanish entirely jumped ship. "What is the matter, Manuelita?"

"Is... is... Gilberto."

"What happened to Gilberto?"

"He come, senor... the man in dark, the clothing dark. The man come and attack him. In the dining room. And I no see or hear, cuz I in cocina."

There is sangre, senor. Too much the blood."

"Manuelita, talk to me now. Gilberto? It's *his* blood?"

"Oh senor, I cannot look. Only what I see from cocina. But the man come in dark." She drew in several long, strangling breaths, which seemed to collide with screams on their way out. "The man he slice… his *throat!*"

JUD AND I TOOK OUR SEPARATE trucks to the Medical Center after I called 911. I also phoned Diane Cordova, asking her to meet us there. You never know when you might need your lawyer at the bedside of a man who's buying your restaurant if you die in the next 12 hours.

It was pretty much against the laws of nature (not to mention of Texas) for Diane to beat us to the hospital coming from her house north of Fort Davis. But she was there at the entrance to the emergency room when Jud and I drove up. I asked her how the hell that was possible.

"I see," she said with a weary grin, "you don't remember that whole thing about the broom?"

I loved our repartee, and there was so much more where that came from—going on two decades of it, in fact. It was what we had now in lieu of wild sex. But haunted by my friend lying close to death and by the man in dark clothing who'd put him there, I didn't have the heart for any of it.

A Presidio County sheriff's deputy was waiting in the, well, waiting room. He rose from his orange plastic chair, one of many planted along the row of windows, and planted himself between us and the front desk.

"Do you folks have business here?" asked the deputy, who, like his compadre killed in this very hospital when they kidnapped Meridyth, seemed hopelessly young and bright, in appearance if not always intellect. At least, to the best of my knowledge, I'd never slept with *his* older sister.

Deputy Horace Jenkins was determined to stand in our way.

We were, of course, a chef, a lawyer and more or less an Indian chief. That might have made a great proposal for *Gilligan's Island: The Next Generation,* but it conferred upon us no legal right to see anyone or do anything. Diane stepped forward, giving the deputy her patented I'm-tough-and-you'd-love-it-with-me smile.

"I demand to see my client, Gilberto Cruz."

Good start, I thought.

Even better, it worked.

We saw Gilberto, as demanded. He was lying on a hospital bed on wheels, in a makeshift room created by four drawn curtains. Doctors and nurses came and went, checking his vital signs and writing numbers and descriptions on several charts. Wrapped around his throat was a thick blanket of gauze, which they changed whenever it went from white to red.

Gilberto wasn't able to talk.

"I tried to tell you that," Jenkins said. "They got him on some real powerful meds."

"What do we know about what happened?" This was Diane, and I figured she was a better asker than I'd be.

"Only what he told me when I first got here."

"You *talked* with him?" This was me, getting excited about hearing something beyond Manuelita's non-narrative.

"Yes, sir. I did. For just a couple minutes." Jenkins pulled a small notebook from the breast pocket beneath his badge and began flipping through. "So... Cruz says he was leaving the restaurant from the kitchen by way of the dining room about 11:10, 11:20 latest. It was dark in the dining room, and he was carrying this leather bag with cash in it."

"For night deposit. At our bank."

"That's what he said, or what I think he said anyway. He kept switching into Mexican."

"Go on."

"Just as he was reaching the front door, which had been locked from inside when the place closed a bit after 10, somebody grabbed him from behind. Hit him a couple times, probably with a fist, he said, then flashed a knife. Cruz said that's where he stops remembering, but he came to on the floor with blood all around him, pouring out of his neck. He said the assailant had gone. All he could hear was a woman screaming."

"That's Manuelita," I said, picturing the hysteria I'd heard her pour into the phone.

"I'll need to talk with her."

"Of course. Just let me know when." This frustrated me more than I dared to admit: knowing that the deputy would let me know, and then I'd let Manuelita know. And then, immigration rules being what they are, there'd be no more Manuelita. She would be missed at Mesquite.

"Why, Deputy?" asked Diane intently. "What do you think happened here?"

"Normally, I'd say it was robbery. You know, goddamn kids trying to score drugs. The usual." Jenkins flipped another couple pages. Not much information could fit on any single page. "In fact, that's what Cruz thought and still thinks, apparently. He told me the guy cut him to get at the money in that bag."

"But there's never much," I broke in. "Nearly all of our business is credit cards."

"I kinda figured that," the deputy said, shutting his notebook. "But that's what he told me. He kept saying 'I'm sorry, I'm sorry.' Over and over, until the docs put him under." Jenkins moved his eyes from me to Jud to Diane, then back to me. "And, well, there's a whole other reason I'm discounting robbery as a motive."

"What's that?"

"The deposit bag was still there when the EMTs showed up, lying right beside Cruz in a big pool of blood. And while we can count the money later, it's a pretty safe bet it was all still there."

I thought about this, and it didn't make me happy. A robbery was one thing. A murder attempt was something else. It pointed darkly toward other things that had entered my life recently, that I'd let into my life in a moment of confusion or weakness, that I wondered how I'd ever drive out again.

After we finished with Jenkins, who said he'd want to question me at my restaurant once the crime scene guys had gone over it, Diane announced to the deputy and everyone else that she needed a cigarette. Diane didn't smoke.

She wanted to talk in private with Jud and me. Her face was grim and drawn and pale, to a degree I'd never seen it. Every ounce of youth had drained out of her, even the ounces that I regularly inserted from memory.

"I have a real bad feeling about this," she said.

"They said they think he'll pull through."

"Yeah, they said that. And that's a blessing. But that's not what's bothering me."

"What is, Diane?" This was Jud, who over the years had adopted her as his attorney, his little sister and his friend—without any of our glistening back story from college, I'm relieved to report.

"Something's just wrong" She rustled through her purse, and for a moment I thought she *was* searching for a smoke. But all she dredged up was a bent and dirty loose stick of Fruit Stripe gum. Unwrapping it quickly, she slammed the multi-colored stick hard into her mouth. "There's no reason," she chewed, "for this."

"Does there have to be a reason? I hear a lot of crimes…"

"Listen, Brett. A lot of crimes don't make sense. And a lot of reasons don't make sense, especially when stupid, crooked or insane defendants start spouting them in front of a judge and jury. But honestly, yes, crimes almost always happen for a reason."

"And the robbery thing doesn't wash?"

"Nope," she said. "It's like someone was trying to punish Gilberto, or teach him a lesson. Maybe give him a message."

"For instance: Don't buy my restaurant after I die?"

"I don't know. The timing is scary, so it's hard to let that nagging thought go away. But even then, no offense, but what's the huge deal about a damn restaurant? It's not like it means all that much."

"I understand, Diane."

"So, it's like… it's like there's something Gilberto or maybe somebody else he knows is about to do, and somebody *really* doesn't want them to do it. This is their way of telling you so."

Jud and I looked at each other, about as close to speechless as either of us ever gets.

After a while, standing exhausted outside in the driveway just beyond the reach of the light, it felt like there was nothing left to say. Diane had told us what she wanted to, and Jud and I couldn't tell her anything at all without telling her too much. With silent agreement all around, we went back in and gave our closing thoughts to Deputy Jenkins. We all took his card and gave him our cell phone numbers, promising to reconnect when things made more sense. I wondered when the hell that would ever be.

Still, as Diane and Jud turned toward the exit, I asked them to wait for me. I motioned toward the pulled perimeter of curtains and Jenkins gave me his permission for one quick glimpse inside.

With the screen pulled behind me and Gilberto at peace on that hospital bed, I understood again how little people ever really say to each other. It was crazy for me to worry that he would die, when all the doctors had promised he wouldn't, but I worried anyway. It was crazy to worry I'd never again see his dark, muscular, 4-foot-10 towering beneath me, for towering is what it seemed to do, but I worried anyway.

And it was crazy to worry that I'd never figure out what he said or did that made 12 dark-skinned, often-frightened people work harder for almost no money than any 25—no, make that any 30—of my kind ever would or could, no matter how much I offered to pay them. But I worried about that anyway too.

Touching the sheet that covered Gilberto and clinching my eyes tight shut, I prayed every prayer I ever remembered to every rendition of God I'd ever heard of.

"*Jefe?*"

At first I didn't budge, certain I'd heard nothing and then resisting what surely was somebody coming to shoo me the hell away. Or maybe it was the voice of the Almighty. Speaking broken Spanish-English, no less.

"Hey, *Jefe.*"

Opening my eyes, I saw that Gilberto had somehow wriggled out of the oxygen mask that covered his mouth. His lips looked dry and kept sticking together, but they were moving, sometimes without producing any sound. And his eyes were open, though not to any consistent degree.

"G, can you talk?"

He nodded.

"They say you gonna make it, G. You gonna make it."

"Si, jefe." He struggled at first, but talking seemed to get a little easier as he kept pushing at it. "I know."

"The doctor tell you?"

"No. The man… who did this… *he* tell me."

"What?"

"He say…" Gilberto shook his head side to side as though to decline something, but it was only to free his mouth completely from the mask. "He say he no cut me too deep. So I could tell to you."

"Who was it, G? Do you know who did this?"

"He say… he come, jefe, from Victor Morales."

"Morales?"

"Si. And he say he want me to tell my boss one word from him, and you better listen. Solamente, jefe."

"One word? What word?"

"Yes," Gilberto said. *"Stop."*

THE RUMPLED GRAY BRIM of Jud Garcia's hat was encircled by a chain of small, interlocking, sun-bleached chicken bones. The hat looked like it just came from Popeyes.

"Why *not* chicken bones?" Jud said, pressing it down onto his twin black braids. "It's my good hat."

"So where's your war paint?"

"Not really necessary."

"I'm surprised."

"Like all of the three whole Jews I've known in my life, you might say I'm Reformed."

All morning long, after about three hours sleep at our respective domiciles (legal language, thank you, Diane), Jud and I had tried to talk ourselves out of it. But no matter what we said, did or thought, we couldn't. Enrique wasn't going to buy any excuse, not without retribution. And I couldn't help noticing that, even though we were taking my Cherokee most of the way to that ranch outside Terlingua, all the weaponry Jud had picked out the night before had disappeared.

"Already there," he said cryptically. "Everything is already there."

"Not you and me."

"Yeah, there is them guys."

Failing to come up with a better plan, we climbed into my Cherokee and drove for close to two hours, initially east on old Highway 90 into Alpine past Reata, the first restaurant to make anybody think twice about food around here, and then down 118 as far as Study Butte.

Almost as soon as you make the turn south, the last semblance of what seems civilization fades quickly. In this part of Texas, leading down to Big Bend and the Rio Grande, you think nothing of driving 30 or 45 minutes without seeing anything human. And you grow accustomed to climbing slowly upward over the highway's next rise for a magnificent view of absolutely nothing.

"Nice buttes," Jud said at one point.

"Thanks for noticing."

At Study Butte, with its merest suggestion of human enterprise—motel, gas station, café, all pretty much the same building—we turned west on a much smaller road. The terrain got angry, or maybe just tortured, and I began to wonder if even my four-wheel drive would be drive enough.

There was dust piled along the side of the road, with a strong wind blowing through the canyons that didn't want to leave it there.

"Terlingua," Jud said.

For those chili cook-offs the first Saturday in November, I'd read, 20,000 or more gathered around this non-town of a town, sleeping at night mostly in their cars or on the ground beside their Harleys. The place was

Key West without any water, with each rusty old Airstream doing its best to look permanent with a fence or a lean-to—all things, by the look of them, constructed from leftovers to support the intrepid pursuit of beer.

We pulled off the curvy road at one especially sand-blown patch, drawn in by the sight of seven would-be cowpokes with salt-and-pepper ponytails sipping from mugs around a stone pit. The fire had burnt down on the way to out, but the day was turning hot anyway. Flannel jackets and overshirts had been shed by the cowboys, lying in heaps like modern art all over the dry ground.

"You're kinda late for coffee," offered the solid blonde woman who came out of the bright pink trailer. "But you're kinda early for barbecue." She made as to slap her forehead as the three of us stood facing each other. "My, where have all my manners gone? I'm Kathy the Kosmic Kowgirl."

"Hi, darlin'," said Jud, shaking her hand roughly, deciding this one would have to be his. "You from around here?"

"Now you're a big one, aren't you?"

"That's the rumor, yes. It's a good thing I'm so shy."

"And yes, I'm from around here. As you can see, this is the place to be in Terlingua. If there ever could be such a thing. It's where the FedEx guy drops packages for everybody in town. One, he can actually find me instead of these folks, who pretty much live under the rocks." She nodded affectionately toward her ponytailed cowboys. "And two, he's less likely to get shot."

The three of us laughed.

"So Kosmic Kathy, you know the old Macmillan ranch, don't you? Up on the mesa, east of town?"

"Sure, who doesn't." She giggled. "Oh a lot of folks don't, I suppose. But yeah. Nobody been out there in years, though. Like maybe the '60s. Then again, who can remember those?"

"You have a point."

"You boys headin' out that way?"

"Nah," Jud said. "Just makin' friendly conversation."

Before it was over, Kathy did coax a little more semi-solid coffee out of her machinery and then stepped into a separate pink shed to check on her brisket, sausage and ribs smoking over wood. Any other time, as a chef, I would have talked to Kathy for hours about what wood she used, about her dry rub, about time and temperature. Yes, *definitely* any other time.

Jud and I said nothing to anyone around the fire pit as we sipped, and they all seemed content enough with that arrangement.

In appropriate tribute to the town's inhabitants, the land beyond Terlingua is psychedelic. Rock clusters tossing purple shadows tilt toward you as you climb, then snake back the other way as you tumble, down to the desert floor a thousand versions of brown, ebony and gray. Sometimes gazing over an edge, which you'd be advised never to do, you see a universe covered in pebbles—only to realize they're giant boulders really far away. This, I caught myself thinking in silence, is much too beautiful a country to never see again.

About halfway up the switchback to the old Macmillan ranch, Jud motioned me to the side.

"I think this is my stop," he said, which is exactly all it turned out to be. There was no real place to pull over.

"What will take you to the top, Jud?"

"Injun trails. Naturally."

"How?"

"That, sir," he deadpanned, "would have to be my line."

And I was alone.

For the final four hundred yards of switchback before the crest, I had to shift the Cherokee into second gear. The trail—since any memories of "road" seemed a long time ago—turned steeper than anything I'd ever driven on, and parts of it were washed away by decades of rain and inattention. At times, a large section would crumble and drop away as I climbed, just to make the unwelcome point.

I greeted my arrival at the place I'd been told to park with relief. And then, quickly, I corrected myself.

The location both was and wasn't as Enrique had described it. There, off to my right looking south toward the green snake of the Rio Grande, was the abandoned house, small and built of dark brown wood that had not held up. Most of the windows were broken out, and there was a hole in the roof—though what would have flown all the way up here to crash down through it was beyond me.

And to my left was the abandoned barn, in better shape than the house, a hulking wood structure with most of its huge double doors intact beneath a window or opening high up for loading hay.

Even growing up in West Texas, I was ill-prepared for the vastness of this space. With sun burning the top of my head and wind roaring in my ears, I gazed around at a flat but slanting surface larger than a football field, with what seemed to be sheer cliffs dropping off on every side. A hundred feet or so in front of the barn, a wooden settler wagon slumped in disrepair, dipping badly at the corner where one wheel was taking a siesta. Tiny purple and blue flowers had sprung up between the spokes in the dust.

Nothing moved. There was no sound except the wind.

Gripping the empty briefcase tightly in my left hand, I moved forward, taking each step and then checking to make sure I was still alive. I got as far as the old wagon, closer to the barn than to my Jeep, when I decided to say hello.

"Enrique!" I shouted.

At the bottom of a canyon, your voice is huge, echoing its way into eternity. At the top of a mesa, your voice is tiny. My shout seemed no more than a whimper, and instantly it was gone.

"Enrique Morgan! It's me, Brett Baldwin!"

There was nothing for a long minute, then a deep groan from one of the barn doors as someone pushed it open a few inches. And then a few inches more. I watched as it opened into dark shadows, and then as the shadows filled with a man.

Enrique looked much as I remembered him, dark and wiry, a bit like a Mexican but taller. His bulk had increased since I last saw him, though, all muscle and no fat, surely a result of years lifting weights in prison. Everybody I've known who's gone to prison ends up in better shape than I am. The arms emerging from his short-sleeved workshirt were covered with tattoos.

"Howdy," Enrique said, instinctively patting the machine gun hanging at his side. "Glad you could join our party."

Maybe those words were his command, or maybe he did something else, but just behind me to the right I heard the front door of the house spring open and a line of men with machine guns file out. The first of the men walked directly toward me. The rest fanned out on either side, making sure I had no way to escape.

"I'm sure you wouldn't be packing," said Enrique. "But we better make sure anyway. Paco, give the man a good going-over now. And check him for wires while you're at it. I don't want the goddamn FBI or DEA listening in."

I've had sex that was less intimate.

Paco waved when he was through and Enrique smiled. It was a tired smile, I thought, like it was the end of something, a long road. But then again, everything we do in this life is the end of a long road.

"So," Enrique said, stepping farther out from the doorway. "I see you've brought me something."

"Yes, as agreed. No problem getting the money."

"Good. No, Brett, that is excellent. I trust I can come and take that case from your hand now, considering we have so many, uh, friendly witnesses."

"Not yet, Enrique."

"What?"

"The deal, man. That's not the deal. You're going to give me Meridyth and that doctor, before I give you a dime."

Enrique laughed.

"Ah yes. The little show. The little cowboy movie. Well, sure. Why, the hell not?"

To quote Diane at the hospital less than 12 hours earlier, I was getting a very bad feeling about this. Our brilliant plan that had Jud off somewhere waiting to ride in like the cavalry sounded more insane by the second. If my friend wasn't already dead.

Two of the armed men disappeared into the barn and then walked out, one holding Meridyth's arms behind her and the other holding the doctor. Meridyth actually looked better, healthier, than when I'd last seen her, with no IV trailing, only patches of bandage on her arms.

"Thank you, Brett. I knew you'd come."

"And my sister's telling you the truth. She *did* know you'd come. And that's why we were able to do all this."

"What do you mean?"

"It's always the same with the pretty girl, isn't it?" Enrique answered, grinning.

I felt seriously deficient in my understanding of what was going on here, and I didn't like that at all. The guys with guns obviously didn't care, the doctor from India didn't know, and Enrique showed less than deep interest himself. So it was left to Meridyth to drag her handler toward me so we could talk.

"Brett, it's not what you think. We never really wanted anybody to get hurt."

"She's speaking for herself there," corrected Enrique.

"You see, Brett, when my brother made his deal with the feds, he agreed to do some things, to give them people. All that *will* happen, Brett. My brother is true to his word."

"I'm sure," I said.

"But he had one mission, one mission only, from the day he became a free man." Meridyth glanced at her brother. "Get Victor Morales. Stop him. End him. Kill him."

"Meridyth, get real. Your brother was a Morales *guy!*"

"Yes, he *was*. In the past. But then something happened, something terrible." She looked at Enrique again, but his unblinking eyes stared straight ahead. "And he swore, even as they took him to prison, that he would find a way. Don't you see, Brett? The money you brought us will *be* that way. A way to put Victor Morales down!"

I clung to the empty briefcase. My hand had soaked the worn leather handle with my sweat.

"So Meridyth, what you asked me to do here... was fund a drug war?"

"Some will say so, yes. But I was the one, Brett, the one who thought of it. I was the one who realized that the greatest chance Enrique had of getting the money he needed—was *me*. How would he know about Hollywood? How would he know about the insurance money?"

"*Your* idea." It was a statement, not a question. And with it, I felt all the violence of the past few days well up and push me past any place I was used to being. "So this *idea* of yours is why—let's see—why your bodyguard and driver are dead, why a sheriff's deputy with a pregnant wife is dead, why my sous chef is lying in a hospital with his throat cut? Babe, that's some kind of *idea* you had there."

"Don't be hard on me. We didn't know how it would be. We could only try." She smiled, but I think what I saw was desperation. "Look at these burns, Brett." She turned her arms to show me. "We didn't plan on these. And they hurt. And so will the surgery to fix the scars."

"At least," I said bitterly, "surgery *can* fix them."

"That's enough!" Enrique said, breaking his glare. "We need to conclude our business here, Mr. Baldwin. I got places to go—and people to kill."

"Isn't it wonderful, Brett?" breathed Meridyth. "This $15 million will do so much good. Just think of all the billions spent in Hollywood that don't do any good at all."

"My dear sister," said Enrique. "You seem to have missed reading a scene or two. And of course, you told me how in the movies, they shoot all the scenes out of order." He turned to me. "Brett, would you please set that briefcase on the ground and pop it open so it faces us?"

"But—"

"Do it. Now."

With the reluctance I might reserve for stepping off a cliff, I squatted in that mesa dust with the wind howling, undid the latches on either side and lifted open the lid. For a crazy instant, I hoped that some Las Vegas magician had filled the case with $15 million when the audience was looking someplace else. Or at least with that shotgun Jud had picked out for me. The case was still empty.

"What?" This was Meridyth. "Brett, how could—"

"It's all right, my sister," said Enrique. "We're off to a pretty good start in our fundraising. At least some of the money is in the *bank,* with more on the way."

"What?" This time it was my turn.

"You see, we needed you for one reason, Mr. Baldwin. To make it all look legit. And of course, to placate my dear, confused sister here." Though my eyes were drilled to Enrique's, I caught a glimpse of Meridyth struggling angrily with the man holding her in place. "Truth is, Brett, you have almost completed your role with us, and you've done a picture-perfect job. But you got to understand. And for that you need to see one more person."

Something horrible and unwanted tightened in the pit of my stomach as Enrique turned back to that open barn door. Out from the floating dust and shadows walked a tall, graceful man in yet another tailored silk suit, his color-coded silk shirt pressed open at his well-tanned neck.

"Talley?"

"In a manner of speaking," the man said. "It would seem that, as before, I have been a tad less than totally honest with you."

THAT WAS WHEN THE FIRST of Jud's explosions erupted, tearing the back off the mesa like Samson pulling down the temple. As the old joke invariably goes, you have to get their attention first.

Explosions two and three shredded tons of rock on the cliff's front face, turning around some of the armed men as they were racing to see what had happened the first time. One poor fellow even fell down miserably, his machine gun clattering across the ground in the blinding swirl of dust and smoke.

"Aaayyyiiieee!"

The sound roared from deep in Jud's throat as he came up over an impossible rise in what looked like a dune buggy from summer vacation in

Fallujah, one hand on the steering wheel, the other blazing the Bushmaster into anything still able to walk, stand or crawl.

"Come on!" I shouted to Meridyth. And since her handler had run to join his buddies, she could. "You too!"

The Indian doctor was looking stupid, frozen in the middle of all this in his dirty white lab coat. I pressed them into the dust beside the old wagon and yanked the whole thing over on top of them. It was anything but bulletproof, but it was better than nothing.

Jud roared past me in the dune buggy, swerving wildly, and for a second I feared he'd lost control of it. Oh me of little faith. Reaching onto the seat beside him while keeping his other hand on the wheel, he tossed something into the air in my direction, something large and dark and angular.

"Catch!" he shouted.

The Remington 870 TAC floated into my arms. It was a good catch, I thought. But an even better throw.

I pumped the gun once, remembering how from somewhere, and fired in between two guys who were drawing a bead on Jud in his dune buggy. Both of them went to the ground. And so did I, driven by the recoil. But at least I could get back up.

Talley had disappeared into the barn, not surprisingly. Probably had his designer hair buried in the hay. Enrique had taken up behind a boulder outside the double doors, firing at Jud, at me, at the whole world, with his machine gun. I'm sure he hit some of his own guys too, but it didn't look like he cared much.

Explosions four and five came at us then, from behind the ranch house and the barn. These blasts were different, sounded different, splintering wood instead of stone, and driving flames through the heart of each structure like they were the driest fireplace kindling you ever saw. Orange-yellow fire poured out through every opening, and it tore a few openings of its own.

As the surviving enemy began to organize in a jagged circle around him, Jud rolled the dune buggy into a dust-flinging heap and jumped behind it, firing the Smith & Wesson with his left hand and the Glock with his right faster than I could have even pulled them from their holsters. Men went down screaming on every side, they and their weapons thudding to earth like ducks on a November morning.

I was firing too. I think I was hitting people. Over my shoulder, I checked the overturned wagon. Meridyth and the doctor seemed safe. Nobody was paying any attention to them.

There was a hum I picked out then, from somewhere on the far side of the house in flames, the kind of deep, throbbing, pulsing force that sucks the breath out of your lungs by way of your mouth and ears. Excitedly I glanced over at Jud, who was still firing from behind the dune buggy, to enjoy whatever serious mayhem my friend had cooked up next.

His eyes were already on me, though. And they carried a look I hadn't seen in them before. Pressed for a label, I'd say it was fear.

One at a time, through smoke and gunfire, Enrique and his men noticed the hum too, and they spun this way and that wildly with their guns, trying to aim at whatever it was. A few let off bursts in different directions, lured into doing so by echoes circling upward from the desert floor.

"Down!" shouted Jud. He and I hit the dirt.

From opposite ends of the cliff to the south, two huge military-type helicopters rose up—I saw them from my spot, my shotgun at the end of my outstretched right arm. The sides of the helicopters were open wide, and from them men in dark clothing began firing as soon as they cleared the ridge.

Enrique and his men fell to the ground but repeatedly rose up again, sideways or even upside down, tossed and torn as they were strafed from the air. And then, in the silence that eventually came to rest over the massacre, one copter hovered to cover the action while the other settled onto the dirt. Commandos rolled out the open door and searched the area quickly, thoroughly, not the least bit interested in Jud, me or any other possible survivors.

I heard a shout then and turned to see one of the commandos lifting up the old wagon. Two others raced up, shoved the blood-spattered doctor's corpse aside like a blanket they didn't need anymore and lifted a very alive Meridyth into their arms. They carried her as though weightless, one arm hanging, her mouth wide in an inaudible scream, her clothes splattered with the doctor's blood.

Other men reached to pull her inside, then everyone jumped aboard, and the copter lifted off, joining its partner in a throbbing race toward the green line of river where the United States legally if not always morally breathed its last.

"Aahhaahhh!"

It was a cry of agony, but not only the physical kind. As Jud and I rose from the ground, we zeroed in on its source: a freshly shredded rendition of Enrique, lying in a hump of blood, bone and torn flesh.

"Morales!!"

We ran to him, wishing we still had a live doctor. But it didn't require an MD to see that Enrique was beyond all help. One of his legs and one of his arms had been severed, or nearly so, now held in place around his mangled form by whatever pieces of muscle made it through the assault.

"Goddamn you to hell, Morales!!"

Jud and I squatted close. Jud quickly peeled off his vest, rolled it into a pillow and positioned it gently under Enrique's head. The man nodded his gratitude.

"He killed her," Enrique said.

And in my hysterical pursuit of some silly bit of hope, I sputtered out, "No, Enrique. Your sister will be fine. Somebody will rescue her. No one killed Meridyth."

He shook his head side to side, ignoring the agony that each shake delivered.

"No, you don't understand." After all that had happened today, that was still apparently my lot in life. "It isn't my sister Morales killed. Don't you remember that truck near the border? That truck full of dead illegals?" Enrique drew three deep, gurgling breaths, finding strength for what would prove his final words. "That was *them.* Victor Morales killed my wife and my baby!"

"HEY BOY," SAID JOHNNY LEE CROW, "are you *listenin'* to me'?"

Actually, I wasn't. I was buried deep in a long series of nightmares that made me sweat and scream, even if no one watching me would have noticed. I was being held down and deprived of air. I was being held down and drowned in water. I was being held down and devoured by fire. Always held down. And always with no way out.

"Boy, I said wake up!"

"Huh?" I began eloquently, rising from the nightmares so rapidly that I probably should have gotten the bends. "Oh my God, my God, where am I?"

"Shit," offered Johnny Lee, ever the consoler. "You're just right the hell back in Presidio County Jail."

Looking around, I didn't recognize the place. Instead of the large holding pen I remembered sharing with the Mexican and Billy Crabb Duncan, I was locked in a private cell, with a bunk for sleeping and a Spartan commode in the far corner. Johnny Lee was draped backward over a folding chair inside my cell, his boots planted flat to the concrete only inches from my bunk.

"Let me tell you something, boy," he said. "This time you really outdone yourself, ya hear me? You and that crazy Injun both."

"What do you mean?"

"The next time you two wanna murder 37 people in cold blood, I'd appreciate you pickin' a more convenient place to do it."

It all came back to me now, fact separating in stages from nightmare. The top of that mesa. Enrique and Meridyth. The helicopters rising, cutting down everything in their sight.

"37, Johnny Lee?"

"Yeah, we figured we'd better count 'em. To know how many murder charges to file against you assholes." I think he laughed, but maybe he was just being Johnny Lee. "Personally, I wanna go for first-degree and a date with the needle in Huntsville. But this damn thing might be just friggin' weird enough to keep you at murder two."

"I didn't kill anybody." This was a lie, of course. But a lie, more and more, fit with my morality of the moment. "I told you what happened. Jud and I both told you, when you and your men finally made it up onto that mesa."

Truth is, we were glad it took them as long as it did. Somebody in Terlingua had reported the gunfire, Johnny Lee explained, proof positive that at least one person in that town was lucid. But the law's delay climbing the difficult switchback had given us a good half-hour to get our story straight.

We'd been approached two days ago by Gaylord Talley of Constellation Films, we told Johnny Lee and his deputies, about a ransom demand from

Meridyth Morgan's kidnappers. Because of my *childhood* friendship with the star, the kidnappers were demanding I deliver the ransom personally, or else they'd kill her. Reluctantly, I had agreed.

Still, Jud had gotten worried about me, so he'd followed—carrying weapons for which he held proper licenses—and then attempted to rescue me once the scene got out of control. At that point, the helicopters came in and killed everybody.

It was not a bad story. And not entirely untrue.

The deputies found no money in the briefcase, so we insisted the guys from the helicopter must have taken it. No, we didn't know how much it was, because I'd been ordered not to open the briefcase. For that information, somebody had better talk to Gaylord Talley, who had been staying at the Paisano Hotel.

"Sure," Johnny Lee said. "We checked that out. The hotel had several departures at about the right time. But no guest was registered as Gaylord Talley. And no guest was registered as being from Los Angeles."

I scratched at my head, not as surprised as I would have been a day or two earlier. "Talley was a liar. And liars lie."

"Liar or not, it sure would be nice for you if we could talk to him right about now."

Johnny Lee sat up stiffer, his large tanned hands draped over the chair back. After a moment of silence, he beat a small drum roll on the metal, drew a loud breath and looked at me intently.

"Well, you wanna hear what I think happened?" the sheriff said. "Even though I ain't got the evidence to prove it yet?"

I shrugged, knowing I was going to hear it anyway.

"I think Enrique Morgan, a convicted drug dealer in the employ of Victor Morales, kidnapped his sister to collect the ransom, which was money from some kind of Hollywood insurance scam. And I think he or his sister talked you into being the go-between, for a cut of the action. And then I think somebody double-crossed somebody as the payoff was going down on that mesa, and Enrique ended up dead and somebody else got the girl and the money. So, cowboy, it might be just the fact that you're the only one I got sitting in front of me. But I say I'm gonna prove that this whole damn thing was your fault."

If his story had been totally ridiculous, I would have laughed it off. But his version was close enough to everything I did know, and there was still way too much I didn't.

"That's not what happened, Sheriff," I said, weakly.

"We'll see about that. And by the way, we're talkin' to your great big Injun friend. You two had better tell the same damn story."

Johnny Lee left my cell, and after a while I was led out to a small bare conference room to meet in private with Diane Cordova. She showed up in jeans and a sleeveless blouse, since she'd been trying to steal a day off with her kids. With me in her life, there'd be no such stealing.

"Jesus Christ, Brett," she said, genuinely frazzled but seeking the inner discipline to do her job. "They're talking about more charges against you than they'd probably file against Osama bin Laden."

"It's crap, Diane. They don't have anything."

"I'll tell you what they have. They have 37 dead bodies. And they have you and Jud with enough weaponry to arm a medium-size Latin American country. And they've got, courtesy of you, one of the biggest bullshit cock-and-bull stories I've heard in all my years of lawyering."

"And that's a lot of cock-and-bull stories?"

"Exactly."

I gave Diane the narrative, carefully tracking the version we'd given to Johnny Lee. I included that Enrique had, just before he died, blamed the helicopter attack on Victor Morales. But I held back the confirmation that he'd been working with the feds to bring some people in the Morales operation to justice.

Why, Diane asked, hadn't I told her any of this was happening when we were together at the hospital? Because, I explained, the kidnappers had threatened to kill Meridyth if we told anyone. And they said they'd be watching us day and night.

"You gotta believe me, Diane. I was scared they'd hurt her."

"Yeah. And I'm scared you were thinking with your wrong body part again."

"I swear," I said. "I thought I'd just bring them the ransom money and be done with it."

"That's not quite," she said, "the way it worked out, is it?"

Diane and I talked about people and things necessary for my life, which of course involved keeping my restaurant open while I saw behind bars. After our earlier phone conversation, she'd put in a call to Rupert Hollingsworth, my old culinary instructor from the Art Institute in Houston. Now retired after a globetrotting career that got him to Houston just in time to lose his shirt in the oil bust of the 1980s, Rupert said why the hell not.

Rupe would travel to Marfa and oversee the replacement of the blood-soaked flooring in the dining room, and then run the place once it reopened until Gilberto was recovered enough to come back to work. He would, in essence, be me.

As for my sous chef, Diane had stopped by the hospital to check on him and found that they'd checked him out already. Gilberto was home in Marfa's small version of the barrio on the wrong side of the tracks, being looked after by his wife and his sister.

"The health insurance said that was it, that was all they'd pay for," Diane reported. "Who the hell buys such cheap-ass health insurance anyway, Brett?"

"Uh, I do."

"And whatever happens, you're now upgrading all the employee's health coverage, yes?"

"Done," I said, wincing. "Too bad I can't afford to improve my own."

And finally, I asked her about Jud. He was bruised and cut up but otherwise unharmed. Being held in another section of the jailhouse. Kept apart from me, she explained, in hopes we could be turned against each other. I felt that was unlikely.

Jud was still in his street clothes, Diane said, dust- and blood-covered though they were. There were simply no orange jumpsuits in the Presidio County jail large enough to cover him. They did take away his belt, his boots with their steel toes, his vest with its metal adornments, and his rumpled hat with its ring of chicken bones. Jud, I gathered, was forlorn about losing the chicken bones.

"He says be strong," Diane reported. "He said I needed to tell you that."

He was right.

In the late afternoon, a call came in on Diane's cell phone: her office advising her of a fax to Fort Davis telling her about a bail hearing arranged a few hundred feet from the place we sat. Being the criminal justice system, she laughed, they'd have found her eventually.

"They're asking for no bail," she said, shaking her head.

"No bail? What does that mean?"

"It means, dear one, that until somebody releases you or convicts you, you'll be stuck in this cell."

For the hearing, I was bound in handcuffs connected by chains around my back and between my legs, forcing me to walk across to the courthouse, well, like a prisoner. Diane said it was pretty harsh, that the county or the feds must be up to something. And as it turned out, at least one of them was.

Judge Herbert Hoover was no relation to the former president, but he seemed old enough to be a secret love child of the same father. Most men (and a few women) in positions of Marfa leadership today can credit Hoover with their teenaged turnarounds, giving thanks for the scary stuff he told them about prison life when they were dragged before him. The good judge took all his cues from the legendary Roy Bean, known in the 19th century as The Law West of the Pecos.

"Why, Brett Baldwin," Hoover said, once Jud and I were securely in place with legal representation at our sides. Diane had sent for one of her law partners from Fort Davis to be there for Jud. "I have to tell you something, son, if you don't mind standin' up a minute there."

I did as instructed, chains notwithstanding.

"I knew your daddy, son. And I didn't think the way he raised you was at all worth a shit." Stopping almost in mid-word, Hoover turned to the court reporter. "Please, Ms. Mangini, be so kind as to strike that last utterance of mine from the record."

"Already recorded as 'inaudible,' Judge."

"Thank you. Now as I was saying, I didn't think much of your father but I've heard nothing but good things about you. Especially since you've been back in town, apparently none the worse for time spent in that awful place called Houston. And I just want you to understand one thing, son: I don't know what the hell you're involved in that's makin' us all be here today."

"Thank you, Judge," I said. "I don't know ei…"

Diane kicked me under the table.

"I appreciate your help as always, Ms. Cordova," Hoover smiled, dismissing me back into my seat.

The judge looked down at the stack of papers on his desk, slipped on his reading glasses with slightly palsied hands and turned to one page, then to another.

"As we know, the county is asking that these two defendants be held without bail. Typically in this judicial district, I'm reluctant to rule that way, since folks around here need to get their work done. And frankly, in my years on this bench, I've seen a whole lot of prosecutors who were all hat and no cattle, if you know what I mean."

This sounded promising, I thought. I thought too soon.

"However, in this particular instance, the charges being discussed are unusually serious. And there's also word that the Justice Department and Homeland Security may chime in too. Now you all know my philosophy on that: I just let those big boys fight it out fair and square. But, bottom line, there's a whole bunch of charges here, and they ain't any of 'em for jaywalkin'.'"

"Your honor, sir," Diane said, rising at our table. She looked up at Hoover, awaiting permission to speak.

"Yes, Ms. Cordova? Do you have something enlightening to add?"

"Perhaps." She glanced down at me, and then at her three yellow pads full of notes. "To my understanding, the primary considerations in a bail hearing are danger to self or others, and risk of flight from prosecution. I see no reason, with these dependants, to fear for the first. And both men operate businesses in this county that would falter badly without their daily attention. And, well, your honor, neither Mr. Baldwin nor Mr. Garcia is what you would call wealthy."

"Thank you for your thoughts, Counselor," the judge said. "Any comments on these issues from the other side?"

"No, your honor. I believe the documents we've provided to the courts speak for themselves."

"Ah, that they so often do these days." Judge Hoover sighed visibly, then slowly rolled his spectacles down from his nose and reached for his gavel. "Bail denied."

It was late—well, maybe not *that* late but after lights-out and I was fast asleep in my cell—when Diane entered with a deputy and called my name till I grumbled awake. I was in the middle of the same old nightmare anyway, so any deliverance from it was welcome. They gathered me from my bunk with some urgency and led me stumbling down the hall to the conference room. The deputy stepped outside.

Two tanned and crewcut men in dark Italian suits were waiting on the other side of the table. We sat. They nodded, waiting for Diane to speak.

"Brett, I think these men have something to say to you. And considering your situation, I think you need to listen."

"Good evening, Mr. Baldwin," the man to my left said. "I'm special agent-in-charge Duncan Mills, and here with me this evening is agent Fred Harris. We're based in Washington, D.C." He flipped out an ID, just like in the movies. "We're with the FBI."

"THERE ARE," MILLS SAID, "many things about our investigation into the Morales crime syndicate that we cannot tell you. But there are a few things that we *can*—the ones that involve you, for instance."

"Me?"

"Potentially, Mr. Baldwin. We invite you to think *potentially* here, and suggest that doing so would be beneficial to your situation." Where did these guys learn to talk like this? "We have roughed in some basic ideas for your attorney, and she has in response made this meeting possible."

"Thanks a *lot,* Diane."

She shrugged, and looked at Mills and Harris apologetically.

"Oh don't worry, Ms. Cordova," Harris said, proving he too had a voice. "Your client is hardly the first over-spoiled, over-educated and over-confident asshole we've ever had to deal with."

"Am *not,*" I responded with impressive maturity.

Mills cleared his throat and I looked at him, which seemed to be the whole point.

"Now it's my turn to play good cop," he said. "We are looking at an unprecedented opportunity, a real breakthrough in the long war we've fought against drugs along our single most vulnerable American border. And with the current practice of Mexican drug lords sending their product with illegal aliens, we have a chance, if you'll excuse the trite phrase, to kill two birds with one stone."

"All this involves me how?" I was uncomfortable with this talk of killing birds.

"That's what we've been watching and learning over the past few days. How would you people put it here in Texas?" He glanced at Harris, sharing what little joke there was. "That's what we been *figgerin'-.*"

"And—"

"As you know, the drug business along the border has become immeasurably lucrative to those who play the game right. And down here, considering the high stakes and the, well, amoral nature of the people we're dealing with, the best way to play the game right is to be the last player alive."

"Like with the cartel in Nuevo Laredo?"

"Precisely. But by no means limited to the competing drug lords there. Or in Juarez across from El Paso either. One Mexican border town lost three police chiefs in as many weeks—until, quite to their credit, nobody would take the job. And while all this may seem a Nuevo Laredo or Juarez problem, it certainly has not been limited to there. Quite a number of killings have taken place around Ojinaga, right across from us. Not coincidentally, homebase to the Morales syndicate." He paused for the clincher. "OJ, I believe you locals call it."

"Yes, OJ. Ojinaga," I said, pronouncing it carefully, reassured somehow that the FBI knew its nickname and bothered to say the Spanish j as an h. "Never been. Though I'm told there's nothing much there."

"No, there isn't. And yes, you might."

"What?"

"You're presumably aware that, in our government's efforts to combat drug and human trafficking, there are many techniques employed. But the holy grail, if you will, has always been getting somebody on the inside. In recent decades, with advancing technologies, the importance of achieving such a coup has only increased."

"And if *that's* where you guys think I come in, you must be kidding me." I glanced, somewhat more hysterically by the moment, toward Diane. But she only nodded my attention back to the FBI.

"What we have now," offered Harris, "and have frankly never had in the past when it comes to the Morales operation, is a connection."

"A link, *potentially*," said Mills, who clearly loved the word. "One we never could have developed on our own but that fell into our laps. It's all part of our parole agreement with Enrique Morgan."

"And that link is?"

"Why, *you*, of course," Harris said. "By way of Enrique's sister, Meridyth Morgan."

"And her, shall we say…" It was Mills this time, "warm feelings toward you."

"Feelings!" I kind of lost it at this point. "What the hell have you guys been smoking in the evidence room? Meridyth doesn't *have* feelings! She's an actress, for Christ's sake!"

The FBI guys nodded to Diane. I guess they could tell I was having what Gaylord Talley would surely have called "a moment." So I stopped having one immediately.

Based on what Mills and Harris told me in the hour that followed, as the clock on the wall ticked past midnight, they had a lot of ears in the right places—and a lot of hands in the right pockets. They had reason to believe, they said, that Meridyth would be contacting me from Mexico soon, supposedly on the basis of her affection for me but, more pointedly, as a way of reaching out to me on behalf of the Morales group. Their motive for this outreach was, so far at least, unknown.

Anything Meridyth said, I was to agree with. Anything she suggested, I was to do. I couldn't help thinking (and so, of course, saying) that the whole thing sounded way too much like marriage.

"A marriage of convenience," snickered Mills. "Like most in our line of work."

What the FBI wanted me to do sounded simple enough, if you ignored about 12 million unknowns. I would wait for the phone call from Meridyth that they had "solid information" was coming soon, and we'd get down to cases from there. As envisioned, I would accept Meridyth's invitation and travel into Mexico via Ojinaga to meet with the Morales syndicate and negotiate her release—probably meeting with Morales himself.

I, of course, would be wearing surveillance technology seven ways to next Tuesday, most specifically the kind that would produce a studio-quality, virtually Top 40 recording of everything we said. Hopefully, what we said would be enough for the U.S. to seek extradition. Or, even better, to pick up Morales and put him on trial the minute his feet again touched American soil.

It was, of course, the 12 million unknowns that bothered me. Nobody could know what Morales would be after in this deal: if it would be as straightforward as money, or some other thing that might be more sinister.

And no matter what Morales wanted, one fact continued to haunt me more than all others put together. The last fellow to make a deal with these same FBI agents, Enrique Morgan, was now lying in the Presidio County morgue, with an arm and a leg shot off.

What the FBI was offering me in return was even simpler: my freedom. They would essentially put my prosecution on ice and I would be free to resume my life, pending the satisfactory completion of our arrangement.

"And Johnny Lee Crow," I had to ask. "He can't be too happy with what you guys are trying to pull off here."

"Actually," Mills said, "we haven't informed the Presidio County sheriff as yet."

Harris pulled a pair of documents out of his briefcase, matter-of-factly describing them as a cooperation agreement outlining our plans—without, naturally, outlining any of our plans—and a release agreement letting me walk. The latter was already signed by Judge Herbert Hoover, the self-proclaimed law west of the Pecos.

"And by the way," offered Mills, "I kinda feel bad about putting the squeeze on you in court today. I mean, all that talk about terrorism and Homeland Security. It was all I could do not to mention sending you to Guantanamo. But as my Daddy used to put it, you gotta get their attention first."

I looked at Mills in a questioning way, and his near-perfect FBI composure caved.

"OK, you caught me." Mills was grinning at me. "My Daddy was Joe Texan, and I was born down here too. He was in the Bureau, and he moved our family from Odessa to Washington as part of LBJ's administration, right after the Kennedy assassination. Those were some wild times, let me tell you."

"You know, Mills," said Diane, "I'm beginning to like you better already."

"And how about you, Harris," I asked. "Are *all* of you guys actually from Texas? You've just suppressed the accent?"

"Nah, not me." The accent he slipped into made the rest of his answer unnecessary. "Cambridge, Mass."

"Pity," I said.

With Diane reading over my shoulder, we assessed the documents set before us. Everything seemed in order legally, she said, from the presence of Judge Hoover to the absence of Johnny Lee Crow. I asked for a pen, and not surprisingly, Harris had one waiting for me.

"I'll sign this," I said, locking on their eyes a final time, "on one condition."

"God, what *now?*"

"I'm not leaving here if Jud's Garcia's not leaving here."

I wasn't sure exactly what to expect from our nation's top cops, but I certainly wasn't expecting the near-hilarity that overtook agents Mills and Harris at that moment.

"The documents for Mr. Garcia's release," said Harris, "are already in the works. And I really have to hand it to you two. You're either amazingly loyal or extremely stupid."

"Yes," Mills said. "We enjoyed a pleasant conversation with your oversized native American accomplice. And he told us all the same damn lies you did."

EINSTEIN MAY HAVE PROVEN all things relative, but where I come from, Meridyth's call to my cell phone the next morning must have fit the FBI's official definition of "soon."

"Hello, Brett. It's me."

The tone and vocabulary were intimate, trusting, and maybe a tad resigned. With a single word, that last one, Meridyth Morgan included me in what I hoped was the short list of people expected to recognize her voice without question.

I was sitting in my office at Mesquite when she called, trying to figure out where to start. Rupert Hollingsworth had come to Marfa anyway, despite my being released from jail. There'd be enough work for two or even three chefs filling in for Gilberto, he insisted. At the moment, he was out in the dining room keeping the installers honest with the new wood flooring where my sous chef had fallen.

A blessing, really. I'd seen enough spilled blood to last me a lifetime.

"Always delighted to help," Rupert had said, his working-class London accent still intact after 42 years away, "a culinary student who makes me look so bloody good."

"Meridyth," I said into the phone, lifting my right boot and using it to kick the door shut. "How are you? Where are you?"

"I'm here, my dear friend. In Mexico. I suppose you'd say I'm a prisoner, but I'm being treated well enough. Happily, I'm worth most to the people who took me when I'm all in one piece."

"Thank God for that."

"Indeed. But Brett, I have to tell you something. They've asked me to call you." She was sharing a confidence. She shared a confidence well. "To set up a meeting, about getting you down here. They want to talk with you, honey, about…" She suddenly sounded close to tears. "About coming here to take me home."

I had already pressed the button on my desk that alerted my FBI listeners—just an alert, mind you, since every single conversation I had that day was being recorded already. There would be, therefore, a lot of taped hours devoted to the price of king salmon on the dock somewhere near Seattle. A green light assured me that my exchange with Meridyth was being saved for posterity in the digital universe.

"Tell me," I said. "What do you need me to do?"

After hanging up, I spent the next four hours in my office, grasping at every moment in my restaurant as the miracle I now knew it was. Like Scrooge on Christmas morning, I struggled with how much to pay the staff while we were closed, and then gave up and put in for their entire paychecks. And I made a note to visit with one or more agents about improving their health insurance as soon as I got back from Mexico.

If I got back from Mexico.

Pressing such concerns aside, I turned to creating a special for the first night we were open. That process worked just like it always does—and surprised me just like it always does.

There I was, thinking about smoked wild boar short ribs with an Asian-tinged, orange-zested barbecue sauce, or maybe instead serving some kind of polenta. So, of course, in my tortured brain, the ribs ended up tumbling *onto* the polenta, which would also get a swift kick in the butt from chopped jalapeno and Monterrey Jack cheese.

Excited by what all this genius might taste like, I invited Rupe in from his grim task for a practice run. It was essential in chefdom that he make the dish exactly the way I wanted it, even when we both knew he could make something on his own that was three times better.

"Hey chef," Rupe said, stirring the pot of bubbling polenta over flames that leaped up at his fingers on all sides. "You know what the old-timers always said, right?"

"No, what?"

"Sell it for 50 cents at breakfast and it's grits. Sell it for $19.50 at dinner—and it's polenta!"

That moment with Rupe in my kitchen, with its heat and nerves and shared laughter, was all it took to carry me back to and make me long for my earliest days as a chef.

He'd been teaching during the day at the Institute, facing a gang of no-talent, no-energy post-teens like me, while also working the hot line nights at Brennan's of Houston. This, of course, was years before a fire destroyed the historic building and severely burned an employee and his four-year-old daughter who'd sought shelter from a killer hurricane.

To my surprise, though it probably meant less than I thought it did at the time, Rupe asked me to help out at Brennan's three nights a week.

I was young, white, not-ugly and fairly well-spoken, so the managers all grabbed me up for waiting tables. Still, I proved such a washout as a waiter that Rupe got me in the kitchen after all, sticking me places where I couldn't injure myself or others. Rinsing lettuce was my skill level back then, or slicing up chicken breasts grilled by somebody else to top our group-dining Caesar salads.

"It's a war, you know," Rupe told me one night after work—no, one early morning, as our polyglot band of brothers inhaled pho and beer at a funky downtown Vietnamese joint. "You know about the kitchen, right?"

"Hrmaarnlala," I said, spooning in pho as fast as I could.

"Every night you cook is full-on combat, Brett. And at some point every night in a busy kitchen, you know you're going to die. So then, when you *don't* die, when you survive for one more night, you look around you at the only people who could ever make that possible. And those," Rupe said, sweeping his hand across the dark eyes of Mexicans, Salvadorans, Ecuadorians and Vietnamese at our table, "would be these guys sitting right here."

And then I knew.

I knew more fully than I knew that English, history, philosophy, psychology, geology and sociology were not the majors for me, even though in some long, confused sequence I'd sampled them all. I knew more fully than I knew that the college degree I'd walked off that stage with was so universal, and at the same time so generic, that it prepared me for nothing as perfectly as it prepared me for everything.

I knew that night over bowls of pho, listening to Rupe talk with an increasing slurring of his words, that I had somehow, miraculously stumbled upon my life. And that even after a transplanted and miserable childhood, I knew a true family when I felt one.

Ding! Ding! Ding!

"OK, chef," said Rupe, banging a fork on a dinner plate that held the polenta topped with wild boar short ribs, sauce drizzled over the top and around the edges of the plate. "I'm gonna taste this now."

He did, his teeth tearing a chunk of smoky meat from the long, curving bone and chasing it with a forkful of polenta. He closed his eyes, and a smile slowly formed on his lips.

"That's some real good shit, chef," Rupe said with his mouth full.

My reverie was over.

Agents Mills and Harris were waiting for me in the makeshift HQ they'd set up over several adjacent rooms at the Thunderbird Motel, one of those over-the-top '50s rehabs more elegant now that it ever had been in real life. I hope the FBI hadn't displaced Matthew McConaughey or somebody like that.

One of the rooms they showed me functioned as dorm, cleared of its artsy retro furniture with mats and bedclothes strewn about the floor. The room next door was for monitoring done in shifts, all but a small space in the center filled with wiring, computers and screens.

"Lotta waiting," Harris explained.

We were indeed waiting, for the call from Mexico Meridyth had told me would come at 5. It would come from her, Mills explained confidently, since Morales would want her to remain my focus. As long as I was thinking about her, he could be sure I'd do whatever she told me. Somehow the guy knew me pretty well.

Beyond that, we figured there'd be a meeting set up, with place and time dictated by Morales.

"He's coming to meet me in Marfa?" I asked, suddenly concerned. No, you might better make that scared.

"Hardly. The whole secret to these guys, the way they stay alive, is to keep as many people between you and them as they can. Always. Until the last minute."

"Then *who?*"

"You got me. If we knew that, we'd pick him up now and start beating everything out of him." Mills smiled. "Sorry. Just a little FBI humor. No, you won't know who you're meeting. And if Morales is on top of his game, the guy won't know who's he's meeting either."

"That's some meeting!"

"Listen, Brett," said Mills. "From this point on, nothing's going to work the way you think it should. Guys like Morales, they aren't concerned about progress as we know it—only about puzzle pieces. And in his puzzle, the less the little pieces know, the better."

"Makes them expendable?"

"Hey," Harris clucked to Mills, "I'd say he's catching on."

We waited in the monitoring room, with long stretches of silence punctuated by technology. Every 20 or 30 minutes, an agent would walk up to Mills and Harris with a new piece of equipment to check out that had just arrived via FedEx. Some pieces seemed almost invisible, and any would fit deep in palm of your hand.

"Amazing times," said Harris.

"Yep," chimed Mills, sounding more Texan by the minute.

At five in the afternoon my cell phone vibrated and the room scrambled. In a very real sense, I had nine other guys at the Thunderbird Motel waiting to answer this call.

"Brett, it's Meridyth."

"Yes," I said.

"Morales told me what you need to do."

She gave me a time and a specific place for the following evening, but I hardly had to write any of it down. Three other guys were scribbling in notepads as we spoke, and one wearing ear buds was tapping each word into a keyboard balanced on his lap.

"How will I know who I'm looking for?" I asked Meridyth. Mills nodded approvingly, as he had given me the question earlier.

"You'll be told."

"And if my contact doesn't know who I am, how the hell's he going to tell me?"

"I'm sorry, Brett. That's all Morales said."

Before we broke the connection, Meridyth promised to be waiting for me and I promised to get there as quickly as I could. It wouldn't be long now, she promised. That, I didn't say, was what I was afraid of.

"He's good," said Mills. "Real good."

"Thanks," I beamed.

"Not you, dumbass. Morales."

"Oh."

"Seriously," said Harris. "No wonder we've never laid eyes on this guy."

"Now hold on." This was me again. "You mean you're sending me to meet with some Mexican drug lord when all you've seen of him are photos?"

"No," said Harris. "We're not."

"Fact is," Mills explained, "we've never gotten a single photo of Victor Morales."

"That," said Harris, "is why we're so excited."

Heading out of the Thunderbird alone, I phoned Rupe at the restaurant and told him I had to go away for two or three days. He took the news in stride, and didn't ask any questions that weren't about what he had to accomplish while I was gone.

I'd like him, I said, to bring in the staff before I left so we could give them their paychecks and talk about our reopening after the attack on Gilberto.

"Got their numbers right in front of me," Rupe said. "Meeting at 2?"

"Sure."

"And chef," he said, his sixth sense working overtime. "Where are you going right now?"

"Don't know, really. Home, I guess."

"Then you better get your butt over here. I've cooked up a little dinner."

With Rupe Hollingsworth, a little dinner was never little. He'd found some fresh snapper and crusted it with Texas pecans, then sided the butter-sauteed fillet with sweet potatoes swirled in a brown-sugar praline sauce and crisp-tender haricots verts.

Better than Rupe's menu, though, and even better than the Cotes du

Rhone he pulled from Mesquite's wine cellar, the bastard had invited Jud and Diane. The four of us toasted festively—even Jud, who dinged our glasses at the appropriate moment with a Riedel full of West Texas tap water.

There were a lot of things we might have called dinner on this night, just as there were a lot of reasons I didn't have much to say. But the name that stuck had one meaning to the other three and a different, darker meaning to me. We all agreed it was the Last Supper.

I ARRIVED EARLY FOR THE STAFF meeting, dressed in jeans and a wash-battered white dress shirt with the sleeves rolled up to my elbows. I carried my life's only tuxedo in a battered garment bag that I pulled out only to fly to weddings or funerals. To my relief, neither happened especially often. This time, it was to get me through my meeting at the Blue Agave Center for Fine Arts.

"Wow," said Rupe, eyeing the bag and affecting the Texas accent that he, after more than two decades here, could plaster at will across his own London twang. "You really *are* gettin' outta Dodge, ain't ya?"

"No, not exactly," I said.

Everybody arrived in time, though some showed up with more leeway than others. Rupe had whipped up a sheet pan of grilled shrimp enchiladas and a big bowl of salad to set up across the bar, so any arrival tension was washed over by a general reconnect built around food. Most of the conversation at the three tables we'd shoved together was in impenetrable Spanish.

They were all in attendance except Gilberto, and even he insisted that his small, dark wife Angelina show up in his stead. He was doing better, she told me, having presumably already given a more detailed update in Spanish to everybody else in the dining room.

"He say he miss you guys," said Angelina. "Especially you, jefe."

This, naturally, brought an eruption of snickering and otherwise rude comments from the kitchen crew, many using the delicious obscenities that had served as my introduction to the language of Cervantes when I first started working in kitchens. They all involved one or two body parts, plus usually your mother, in a dizzying array of gymnastic combinations. Kitchen workers could keep a conversation going for hours, relying on little else.

"Tell him, Angelina, that we miss him also."

As people chewed on enchiladas in rich red gravy and guzzled tumblers of sweet tea, I passed out the paychecks. That helped the meeting get going on a positive note, as I knew it would, since many in my crew would be worried.

"Now," I said, standing at the head of the extended table, "there's a few things we need to go over." I looked around at each of the faces I counted on to keep my alive night after night. "I know we've all been through a shock. But Gilberto is going to be fine and will be back at work, according to his doctors, in a week or two. And if we listen to Gilberto, it may be a hell of a lot sooner."

Everybody laughed, especially Angelina.

"The thing is, I have to go out of town for a few days. Personal business, you know." They all knew. "So I've asked my old culinary instructor Rupert Hollingsworth to run the kitchen while I'm gone. He will be Chef Rupe to you."

"Do you absolutely have to use the word *old?*" asked Rupe.

"OK, *former.* He'll create the specials until G gets back. Of course, if there's some idea you want to kick in, see him. Obviously, do what he says just like he's me. I'll be back as soon as I can."

"Regular schedule for Saturday night," Rupe said, rising beside me. "As of now, we don't have any reservations. Nope, not a one. And frankly, guys, we're not gonna beat ourselves to death to get any. Whoever comes in, we feed them, that's all. Then Sunday brunch, and by that point we should be back in the game."

"That's okay," said Paco, Gilberto's totally unofficial second in command. "We back in the game now!"

The staff, those who could anyway, stayed around into the late afternoon—gossiping, catching up on each others kids, and a whole lot of other things that made it seem like they hadn't seen each other in longer than the few days they had.

Garment bag in hand, I made the pre-ordained run by the Thunderbird Motel, letting the FBI wire me for sound and video in ways sometimes even I couldn't see or feel. All this technology was covered by the tuxedo. I think my tux pants were a little tighter than I remember them—but I'm sure that must have been the FBI's equipment.

Then I went off to meet my destiny.

The Blue Agave Center, or simply Blue as it was known around Marfa, had opened on the outskirts of town only a month earlier, and tonight was to be its first big social event. There was an exhibit, of course, but also a fundraiser expected to attract well-to-do cattle ranchers from every corner of Presidio County plus, even more importantly, the new money just in from Los Angeles or New York, Houston and Dallas.

"Have a wonderful evening," the valet told me, taking my still-unwashed Cherokee and zipping it away to a spot between a Mercedes and a Porsche.

Blue was made up of four buildings. The main exhibit hall combined the finer points of a Soho loft and an airplane hanger, a wide, cavernous space of white walls and huge uncovered windows. Behind this building were four smaller ones, featuring large windows and three doors each.

Maybe smaller shows would be hung in there, I thought, once the center found its footing. The number of art galleries and fashion boutiques opening downtown over the last few years, with their attendant cafes and hair salons, implied there was footing to be found.

"Yes, sir. Your name is here." I was handed a pre-printed nametag for my lapel. "Have a wonderful evening, sir."

In the time it took me to plant the adhesive tag on my label, the space between me and the entrance was filled by a seriously oversized albino man in black. The man weighed about as much as Jud did but with, if I were forced to render a medical opinion, absolutely no muscle. It was as if so much semi-solid waste had been poured into a pair of black leotards and a thick, black turtleneck sweater. It was summer in West Texas.

"Good evening, Chef Baldwin," said the vision, tossing his white hair up from his forehead. "I am Clifton Thornhill the Third, owner of the Blue Agave Center for Fine Arts. I bid you welcome!"

"Thank you," I said, accepting his hand.

"I was absolutely delighted to see you listed as a guest of Ms. Morgan's this evening, even though I was crushed that she herself could not be attending in person."

"Me too." He didn't know the half of how "crushed" I was.

"You know, I often have thought that you and I could be kindred spirits when it comes to our appreciation of quality, of the finest things." Thornhill, I decided, had a special snakelike talent for drawing you in, wrapping himself around you till it was too late to get away. "I have dined at Mesquite more than once, and I have always found the experience positively mesmerizing."

"I think," I said, smiling, "we aim for something like that."

"And perhaps we might speak sometime, just you and I, about some ideas I have. They concern merging our talents in some way, to create special events here in Marfa that are second to none in New York, Los Angeles or even…" He paused for dramatic effect. "Las Vegas. Frankly, chef, I was surprised to see that you actually *live* here."

"Of course I live here, Mr. Thornhill. I happen to work here too. Every day. Except the occasional Sunday brunch. You know what chefs say about that, yes?"

"No, what do you people say?"

"Someday, when all the chefs meet again in hell—which is where we all expect to end up—every day for the rest of eternity we'll be working Sunday brunch."

"My, my, sir, that certainly is a good one. And I *do* see your point, about living here, I should say. It's just that in Las Vegas—where I keep my main gallery—that's not how it's typically done. You don't actually expect the chef to *be* in the restaurant."

"Mr. Thornhill, yes, of course we can meet." I smiled, handing him a business card. "But the last time I checked, this was still little ole Marfa, Texas. And we still kinda like to keep our real hands in the real food."

The gallery owner glanced around, in case others were listening. And from the looks on the surrounding circle of faces, they were.

"Isn't this fellow marvelous!" he exuded to the crowd.

"Now, I'm sure you have bigger fish to fry than a cook who actually cooks."

"Yes, of course," Thornhill chuckled, clearly delighted to be him. "But there are so few I can count on to bring their own *fish!*"

I couldn't help noticing the difference between people I knew hailed from around here and those who had shown up more recently. Longtime residents included men in basic tuxedos that fit about as well as mine did, meaning more or less, and women in dresses that passed muster but probably were the only formal outfit they had: long, shiny and slinky.

The new-money people were, of course, the *real* cowboys, men changing out their bowties for string clasped with turquoise (as though this were New Mexico) and women accenting their backless sequined gowns with designer cowboy hats and boots. To those of us who've lived and worked here most or all of our lives, these people were cartoons. And there were getting to be more of them all the time.

"Sir?"

Still scanning the crowd, I started at the sound of the server's voice, especially because it sounded so close behind me. I turned and recognized him immediately.

"David?"

"Oh, Chef Brett."

"Still doing your thing, I see. Catering?"

"Absolutely. This is the coolest job a guy with a Ph.D. in political science can ever get. And as you recall, I'm not somebody who really likes to get up in the morning."

"I remember," I told him, silently adding "or any other time."

"So, chef… a glass of champagne?"

"No thanks, David. But when you get a free moment, I sure could use a great big glass of iced tea."

It was 10 minutes before David returned, carrying a tray with only my glass of iced tea on it, plus what appeared to be a folded sheet of note paper.

"That's for you," David said. "Some guy slipped me $5 to bring it to you."

"Good for you, David. Who?"

"I didn't pay any attention. Except to the hand holding the $5."

"It's good to know," I smiled, "that a few things in this world don't change."

I gathered both items from David's tray, glancing around the space and seeing milling crowds but picking out no one no one looking at me. No one catching my eye. Holding my tea in one hand, I used the other to unfold the paper. The message was short but sweet.

"Small house in back on right," I read aloud, for the benefit of my FBI listeners back at the Thunderbird. "Meet now."

Another waiter floated by, becoming the beneficiary of my long-awaited iced tea. Pushing through the crowd, I picked out an EXIT sign near the rear of the room and did my best to get there.

The stars were shining brightly once the door snapped shut behind me. The night was immense, dusty with stars, strewn as in a single handful from the black mountains on one side to a different set of black mountains on the other. As I moved slowly away from the hall, all that waited for me was silence.

The door to the house was open slightly, and then entirely when I pushed on it. With strips of starlight pouring in through the windows, the interior was a collection of stark contrasts, illuminated crates and boxes hemmed in by large deep patches of shadow.

"Hello!" By this point, I couldn't see any advantage in being mistaken for somebody else. "It's Brett Baldwin. Somebody in here looking for me?"

There was a small noise in the darkness, definitely the sound of someone moving. Someone who knew *how* to move, that is. The briefest shifting of weight, perhaps only from one foot to the other.

"Hey, is anybody here?"

Suddenly, the noise gathered volume as my listener powered toward me, knocking over things in the darkness as he came. My lips stopped moving, lost the ability to move, as I saw the gun emerging from the shadows and then the form of the man aiming it at my heart. And then I heard his voice.

"Goddamn it to hell," snarled Johnny Lee Crow's all-too-familiar voice. "What the hell are *you* doing here?"

The SWAT team came in then, exploding through every door and window.

JOHNNY LEE SAT IN A METAL folding chair, turning his head side to side in his hands.

"How many of you assholes am I gonna have to talk to before I get to one with a lick of sense?"

"We remain ready to talk about this any way you prefer, Sheriff Crow."

This was Agent Mills, who had handled the questioning from the moment we moved out of the house behind the Blue Agave Center to a portable command vehicle that had pulled up alongside.

"We remind you, however," added Harris, "that the U.S. Attorney has been notified of your arrest and is on his way here as we speak. He has been kept up-to-date on the evidence we have gathered against you, as well as on the charges he is prepared to file under federal RICO statutes."

"RICO my ass! Ain't no racketeering here! I told you, I was on a case, that's all. I got a tip about a meeting involving Victor Morales. And after multiple homicides linked to Morales in my county over the past few days, I determined I'd damn well better be here."

"You, of course, will have a chance to explain all that. In a court of law."

The time since Johnny Lee's arrest had taken on such a surreal quality, it was hard to figure out how long it had been. There'd been a brief flare-up when Clifton Thornhill III burst into the command center in all his black-draped bulk, demanding that somebody pay for the SWAT team's damages to his property. Honestly or otherwise, Mills and Harris convinced him that would be no problem for the federal government.

Besides, Harris added, shouldn't Thornhill be outside tending to his guests, calming them down after the commotion and making sure they drank more champagne? Considering that it looked like the good stuff when it passed by me in the hall, I'm not certain how consoling that notion really was.

But Thornhill went away.

There seemed considerable urgency in the agents' appeal to Johnny Lee, just as there was a massive reluctance on his part to say anything of substance before his lawyer got there. Unfortunately, the attorney had been in El Paso on a deposition and was currently speeding his way along the 200 miles between there and here. Had he not been in federal custody, Johnny Lee probably would have arranged an escort. Those, he may well have been thinking, were indeed the good old days.

"Guys, now listen to me here," said Johnny Lee, going out of his way to sound like there'd been some simple misunderstanding. "All you have to do is call one of my deputies. Any one of 'em will tell you what I've been workin' on. I think you can save yourself some embarrassment when all the facts come out."

I kept wondering when somebody was going to ask me to leave. Instead, I'd been given a cup of black coffee in a cardboard cup and pointed to a soft chair nearby.

"Sheriff," said Mills, and I thought for a moment he might drape a supportive arm around Johnny Lee's shoulder. But that moment passed. "So tell us what exactly is your position on this."

"Christ, weren't you all listening the other 14 times?"

"Humor us, all right," Harris said.

"This afternoon a source I've found reliable on previous investigations called me and told me about a meeting tonight. Involving Morales. He didn't have details, but it's hard enough to get these guys to talk in the first place."

"Yes, we know."

"So I came over here, took a pretty thorough look at the reception and then decided to check out the buildings out back. That's when I found *this* guy, who just has a talent for being there when there's trouble." He nodded to me. "And that's when the A-Team came barreling on in, breakin' a shitload of stuff that didn't even have to get broke."

"So that's your complete statement, Sheriff?"

As though the seriousness of his situation finally dawned on him, Johnny Lee ran what he'd just told the FBI back through his mind and apparently didn't find anything damning enough to retract.

"Yeah, sure. Unofficially. I guess so."

Mills and Harris let Johnny Lee stew for a couple minutes as they walked around him in the chair, asking to see a notebook from this or that agent, perusing the pages. They even chatted with me briefly, asking how I was doing, and I still half-expected them to send me home. But they didn't.

"So Sheriff." Mills again. "We're going to give you a name. And you're going to tell us what you know about it. All right?"

"Whatever I know, I'll tell you."

The agents looked at each other one last time before Harris said, "Enrique Morgan."

If Johnny Lee was shocked to hear Enrique's name in this particular context, he covered it quickly. He did clear his throat and reach across to a small table on which an agent had set a cup of water from the tap.

"Sure," said Johnny Lee. "How the hell could I not know him? It was my daddy who sent that boy to prison back when he was sheriff of this county."

"And since you know Enrique, you do know he was released from federal prison, yes?"

"Yep. It didn't make me happy. I figured he'd come to no good. And that's the way it worked out, isn't it?"

"Sheriff Crow," said Harris, "we could play witty backwoods Q&A all night long. But once the U.S. Attorney gets here, your options get fewer and fewer. We take you back to your own jail, walk you in front of all your deputies and the news media, and charge you with racketeering."

"I wish you guys would stop using that word. There's nothing like racketeering in anything I've done tonight."

"You know, Sheriff," offered Mills. "You're right. Tonight, you were investigating a tip from a source." He paused, pressing his face in closer, till it was the only horizon Johnny Lee could see. "But you're going to have a tougher time explaining more than a year's worth of wiretaps on your office phone, your home phone and your cell phone. Or, for that matter, five years of bank transfers into an account identified as yours in the total amount of $1.6 million."

"Or for that matter," said Harris, "transfers adding up to even more than that to your father over his final three years in office."

Johnny Lee said nothing. Yet with each additional allegation, each additional dollar amount or time period, his face seemed to grow paler, losing its near-textbook West Texas tan.

"So," he said after a long silence. "Enrique rolled on me? He had to give them somebody. And damn, all this time I figured it was Morales. But it was *me* all along?"

"Sheriff, we love to get our hands on Mexican drug lords any time we can. But we consider stopping corrupt public officials one of the best things we can do with our time."

"I suppose you have court orders for all this?"

"Yep," said Mills.

Johnny Lee let out a long, tortured breath.

"And if I cooperate with you on this thing, what happens?"

"Better than if you don't," said Harris.

"First thing I want, non-negotiable—you leave my Daddy alone."

"That's asking a lot. I don't know how far we can take this."

"Then no deal. My father is 74 years old. He's got liver cancer. His life is over, you understand me? The next few months are all he's got left. I'm not going to let you screw 'em up."

"You probably can't stop us from screwin' 'em up, Sheriff."

"That's why I'm doing this, to stop you."

"Fair enough."

"So what do you want me to do?"

Mills had a particular talent for saying huge things and making them sound simple. I knew that too well.

"You, Sheriff, are going to give us Victor Morales. Whatever it takes. You will meet with him—as you have in person seven times, on dates that we have in the record. One more time, Sheriff, that's all we ask. Tell him anything, go meet with him, and this time we'll go with you."

"Shit, boys, you know the bastard'll kill my ass in two seconds when he finds out."

"He doesn't have to find out."

"But he will. You don't know this guy." Johnny Lee stopped, pondering the gravity of what he was about to say.

"Yes, but *that's* exactly what we want. That's all we'll accept, in return for leaving your father to live out his life in peace."

Johnny Lee was looking down, as though the world had gone away, his body empty and deflated. There was no more Mills or Harris. No more mobile command post. No more cup of water, no more folding chair. The corners of his eyes had turned shiny, and what I could see of the whites had gone red.

He nodded, finally, with surrender.

"All right," he said.

Phone calls were made, including one to the U.S. Attorney in his car coming to Marfa. At least for the moment, there would be no high-profile arrest, no walk through the television cameras, no news conference in front of the American flag. There was only Johnny Lee, his hands cuffed in front of him.

"So Sheriff," said Mills, "I got one more question."

"Shoot," Johnny Lee said, laughing at the word under his breath.

"Who really sent you here tonight?"

Johnny Lee weighed the consequences of telling, then figured none of it mattered anymore. None of it.

"Morales did. He called me this afternoon. But then again, you know that, if you've tapped all my goddamn phones."

"Of course," said Harris. "We just wanted to hear it from you. You've been set up, my friend. You know that, yes? Morales set you up here tonight. That should make it easier to return the favor."

"Absolutely."

Stepping out of the command center, Johnny Lee moved slowly. I was off to the side as he was led toward a black sedan between two federal agents. A sudden motion caught my eye. Pushing with all his weight, Johnny Lee knocked one agent into the dust and then, in a single motion, grabbed the handgun from the other with both hands and used it to blow away the rear half of his own skull.

By the time Johnny Lee's body hit the ground, the agent left standing was vomiting all over his carefully polished shoes.

THERE WAS SOMETHING ABOUT Johnny Lee's fall, I decided, failing to find sleep for possibly the 4,378th time that night—something about the way his body crumpled and slid downward as soon as its steering mechanism was shot to pieces.

I couldn't stop seeing that moment, every time I closed my eyes. Whenever I slipped even briefly away from consciousness, the whole scene began to unreel again. And I was there.

"God in heaven, please help me," I pleaded.

I think I said it out loud. And even though it was a prayer for me, it was a prayer for Johnny Lee too. And then I thought of Jud, remembering in my starkest moment of clarity why Johnny Lee's fall wouldn't let me sleep.

It was that morning in my mind all over again, when I watched from the fence as Jud moved among the herd. And when that gunshot echoed, it was the bison that crumpled downward, without even realizing it was dead, just the way the sheriff's body had.

Johnny Lee had needed Jud to be there when he killed himself, someone who would say a prayer for animals and ancestors and sprinkle holy water on their spilled blood. Instead, all he'd had was me. And I, I realized all too painfully, hadn't been good for very much.

I wanted so much to call Diane, to tell her everything I'd seen, and to be reassured by what reckoning all of this was somehow legal. But I couldn't call anyone. The FBI had made that clear enough.

Besides, what seemed a lifetime up the highway in Fort Davis, Diane's kids had to be at school in the morning, and she had to get them there before heading to her law office. There was life to be lived, even here in the middle of death. Calling her now would have been too self-centered. Yes, too self-centered even for me.

So I called Jud instead. Jud never slept. Especially at night.

"Hey, bro," he said, a bit too lightly. I knew he was smoking something in his pipe.

"What's in it, Jud?"

"Something good, I'll tell you that. You wine types would say it's the perfect pairing with CNN."

"What?"

"They're reporting on us, bro."

"Johnny Lee?"

"Almost nothing but. Some earthquake in central China—and little ole us. Hey, look, I got more of this shit here if you need some…" There was silence, then he spoke more quietly. "You were there tonight, when it all fell apart, right?"

"Yeah."

"So, it's like they're saying? Drug deal gone bad. Broken up by Johnny

Lee. Bad guys shot him on their way out the door?"

I listened, my mouth dry as desert sand.

"Yep, that's about it."

"I guess you know, then: the U.S. Attorney's holding a news conference in the morning. Commending Johnny Lee for his years of dedicated service."

"Good," I said.

"And bro, listen to this. They got one of them hour-long specials tomorrow night. About Johnny Lee. The murders. The whole drug-war in Nuevo Laredo. Callin' the damn thing 'Bloodbath on the Border.'"

"NL's a long way from here, Jud."

"Somehow, it doesn't seem quite so long anymore," he said.

I slept eventually. I figured it was close to dawn anyway, but I always figured that when I couldn't sleep, and then it never was. I slept fitfully, sneaking past the dreadful vision of one man's body hitting the ground. Sneaking past everything and everybody, until the loud banging at my door dragged me back.

"Jesus Christ," I snarled, rolling out of bed and, as though drunk, struggling to pull my jeans on. I stumbled out into the living room, switching on the lamp after banging my shin on the coffeetable.

I pressed the curtain aside slightly. It was still dark. Not even close to dawn. And barely visible between my ocotillo and Spanish daggers, there was a black sedan parked next to my Cherokee. Its doors were open, its engine running, its headlights carving a tunnel in the dust.

"Who is it?" I shouted.

"Mr. Baldwin, it's the FBI!"

I looked out the window more fully, and there were two crewcut young men in dark suits and ties. One turned the ID in his hand toward me at the window, so I could see it glint in the light.

"We're very sorry, sir."

Everybody talks about the old days, when nobody in Marfa locked their doors. Those days were no more.

"Yes?"

"We were sent here to retrieve you, sir. By Agents Mills and Harris, sir. There's been a development in the case, and you need to be with them when it goes down."

"Jesus," I breathed.

The agents waited on the porch while I slipped my boots on, then pulled a workshirt over my gray T-shirt. I didn't think to grab my MLC from the hat rack. Locking my front door behind me, I followed them down the steps to the black sedan.

Dark, I remember thinking as one of them held the back door for me. Why the hell does it always have to be so damn dark?

I bent to climb into the back seat. The blow came from behind, sending me into another world.

THE WORLD I ENTERED HAD absolutely no light, and the tight adhesive mask that covered my eyes explained why. A similar strip held my lips in place, along with rope binding my hands at the wrists and my feet at the ankles. There was only darkness, set to the rumble and rocking of the car on increasingly pot-holed roads.

I slipped in and out of consciousness as we rode. I can't recall what I dreamed about in the hours that followed, but whatever it was, it was never enough to wake me. That task was handled, rather nicely I might add, by Meridyth Morgan's hands.

"Good morning, Brett," she whispered. And then, sensing my confusion, "It's okay, baby. You're safe here with me now."

The room slowly came into focus, but there wasn't much to focus on. It was a bedroom, and I lay unbound in a spartan bed beneath a crucifix on the wall. Meridyth held a cool damp cloth in her hand. From the slight chill on my face, I could tell she'd been swabbing me back to life.

My back and neck were sore from the drive. But I felt held in place by the bedcovers, by Meridyth sitting beside me, by the sheer emptiness and anonymity of this room.

"Where am I?" The oldest question in the book. Except for maybe *Why?*

"We're with Morales now. At his home." She lowered her voice, as though sharing a confidence. "It's more like a compound, really. I've never been to such a place."

"But Meridyth, are *you* all right?"

"I've been well-treated. In fact, as the days passed and no one hurt me, I came to the conclusion we were all waiting for you."

"For me? I'm not worth anything to them. How *could* I be?"

"I don't know. Apparently you're mistaken."

The wooden door swung open then, allowing a surprisingly tall Mexican in what seemed a military uniform with a machine gun hanging from one shoulder and a machete hanging from the other to step inside. The man had a deep scar along his left cheek and a thick black mustache that threatened to obscure the entire bottom portion of his face.

"I am called Pablo Sanchez, and am the right hand of Victor Morales," the man with the scar said. "I am hoping that the, uh, accommodations are sufficient for your comfort, senor."

I'm not sure, but I think Sanchez leered at Meridyth for an instant, then broke into a grin that, even through the forest of his mustache, revealed a mouth with many missing and yellowed teeth. He nodded at me, as though all things suddenly made sense, and then seemed to stiffen in renewed commitment to a plan that only he could know.

"Si," he breathed.

"Senor Sanchez," I said.

"Commandante," he corrected.

"Commandante Sanchez. I have been kidnapped and brought here against my will. I am a U.S. citizen. I demand to see someone who will arrange or negotiate my safe return as soon as possible."

It was worth a try, but it was all Sanchez could do not to laugh in my face.

"Senor Baldwin, I am very *pleased* for you," he said, moving closer to the bed. "Your citizenship is a wonderful thing, and it buys you—purchases you?—many opportunities. There are others who are not so fortunate."

"I know. Immigration…"

"Ah, senor, you do not know the first thing about immigration. About a border where, on a nice day, I can see mountains in your country calling to me, calling to us all. And the only thing between us, between our two countries, is a little river. Yes?"

"I guess."

"And there on your side is a big American flag, and on our side is a big Mexican flag, both—how you say?—waving in the sunshine. And people pass between those two flags, those two worlds."

I could think of nothing to say. Sanchez looked on intently, waiting, then gave up.

"So, as you say, senor, these are immigration issues. They are things our leaders discuss, for our good, in Washington and Mexico City—and yes, even in our little state of Chihuahua, in the house of our new governor." He smiled. "And we all must wait patiently for the wise men to do the right thing."

With some discomfort, I rolled myself up to sitting, filling the space beside Meridyth.

"So, Commandante. I think this really has nothing to do with me. You know my name, and you probably know what I do."

"You are a chef." He pronounced the hard "ch," as in church, the way the Mexicans do.

"Then tell me this: why the *hell* am I here?"

Sanchez chuckled in a sublimely ugly way, his mustache seeming to brush right and left across the top of his dark chin.

"Si, claro, senor. Victor Morales said it would be always this. This way, I mean. He said you would ask why. But you see, senor, he said you would ask the question. Only he can give you the answer."

Before leaving the room, Sanchez said we would be heading out in one hour. It was Morales' wish, he said, that I prepare dinner for him that evening, and for that, we would need to go shopping in the market in OJ. It seemed an odd wish, but Sanchez wasn't fascinated by my opinions about immigration, dinner or anything else. At least dinner, I thought, was something I could understand.

He pulled the door shut as he left.

"Meridyth," I said, wrapping my right arm around her shoulders. "It was you who brought me here. You have to tell me what this is all about. And you have to tell me what Morales said about getting us out of this place."

"I needed you to come for me, Brett. That's all I knew." She slipped out of my arm and rose to her feet. Starting for the door, she stopped and turned. "Morales has told me *nothing*, I'm afraid. But now that you are here with me, now that you have come as he asked, I believe he will set us free."

Meridyth moved back toward me, close enough to lean down and kiss me warmly, gently, moistly on the lips. I wanted her lips to linger as long as possible.

"Now you, sir," she said, with unexpected shyness. "Get cleaned up. There's glue from that tape in your eyebrows, and that hair of yours is a mess. It sounds like we're going shopping."

Once in the heart of downtown Ojinaga, I thought back to all the bright *paseos* I'd seen in my travels deep into the Mexican interior—the fresh-scrubbed boys and girls circling the square in opposite directions and flirting beneath the watchful gazes of black-dressed widows clucking to each other.

Meridyth and I had chaperones too. Two of them, in fact. Ours were carrying machine guns.

The market was a kaleidoscopic swirl, with fresh produce grown or delivered from God knows where, considering the dryness of the terrain, enveloped in a bizarre assortment of buckets and brooms, embroidered shirts and dresses, and small appliances like toasters and the occasional outdated microwave. One whole table groaned beneath colored pencils and tablets for kids to use in school.

Sanchez had sent us here with armed men; and while I couldn't spot any others around the market, it only made sense that with one careless shot the whole place would erupt into a battlefield. That was how it felt to me, the frivolity traditionally associated with Mexican markets buried beneath a powerful avalanche of fear.

We'd been driven here in an American-made van reinforced with bulletproof glass and armor along the sides. After so much work, the sliding door designed for so many American soccer moms required a professional wrestler to yank it open.

We'd headed out from the house through the compound guarded by men atop walls and towers, and I couldn't help noticing four helicopters like the ones sent against Enrique Morgan splayed across the dirt, surrounded by jeeps and troop transports from several U.S. wars of the past century. At the far end of a dry, open field squatted a clunky old propeller plane, like something you'd picture delivering the mail in the 1930s. It was covered in dust.

"Pollo?" asked the vendor, breaking into my thoughts. "No have the chicken hoy, senor. Tengo, how you say, *bunny.*"

The three small rabbits the vendor showed me at his stall—their skinned bodies on ice, thankfully, though probably not the cleanest ice you ever saw—did look promising. The long border drug wars had taken their toll, and on this day at least, there was little to buy and few who dared come out to buy it.

I took all three rabbits, with a minimum of haggling over price. The vendor seemed pleased.

I don't know what I was thinking—of course, when we do we *ever* know?—but as I was turning away I recognized the figure depicted on the vendor's black T-shirt.

The Mexican in the old black-and white image was riding a horse, pulling him up roughly after a hard ride, yanking the animal's head to the side. The man wore a wide sombrero above a thick mustache that looked nearly as wide, and below that his chest was crisscrossed with bullets in leather straps.

"Ah," I said quietly, even as the name formed in my mind. "Pancho Villa."

"Si senor," he said, his chest puffing out as far as he could make it. "Villa. Un hombre, verdad." He struggled for a word in English, then found it. "The *hero* of the Mexican people."

"Right." I laughed before I could stop myself. "A damn bandito."

"No, senor. A *hero*. He win battle big. Here. In Ojinaga."

"Here?"

"Claro. Aqui. The Battle of Ojinaga. How you say? I'm sorry, my English not so good. "Against? Si, *against* the federales."

"But federales are good, yes?"

"No, senor." The vendor drew a long breath, and I'd swear his darting eyes scanned to entire square to see if anyone was listening. "Es verdad, senor. Federales *always* bad."

Now it was my turn to glance around, picking up with some relief that my bodyguards were busy flirting with Meridyth as she dug through dresses on a faraway table. Definitely out of earshot.

"The federales," I said. "They protect you from bad men." I must have been feeling bold. "Men like… Victor Morales."

The vendor's face changed. Even with no one eavesdropping, his eyes filled with fear. He pumped his hands quickly in front of his chest, as though trying to press down something determined to rise up.

"Please, you must not. He is the padrino."

"Padrino?"

"Si, like the father of the town. Of all the villages. He, how you say, he keep the peace."

"Not the police?"

The man laughed cynically.

"No, senor. Not the police. The padrino."

"We are told," I said, moving closer, "in my country, that Victor Morales is a monster, a murderer. That he will kill anyone who gets in the way of his drugs. That he has killed many."

The vendor's eyes grew wilder. Almost frantic now, he nodded in the direction of the bodyguards. "Those men belong to Morales. Perhaps *you* belong to Morales, senor. I must say nothing."

"No, no. I do not—I do not belong, as you say. I am told there is much violence here. Worse every day. All because you have a padrino."

"No, is better now. Truly. With Morales."

"What could be worse than having a padrino?"

The man lifted his eyes to mine, and they were full of resignation, the sadness of too much acquired wisdom.

"La guerra," he said.

"I don't understand."

"The... *war,*" he said slowly. "Si, now we have one padrino. It was worse... when we had *two!*"

At other stalls in the market along Avenida Trasvina y Retes, squeezed between stacks of bootleg DVDs, poorly built pyramids of boom boxes and smoky taco stands, I found potatoes and tomatoes, onions and sweet peppers, plus what presumably were basil, thyme and rosemary. The herbs came from exotic, unknowable local strains that all looked a bit like marijuana, but their aromas and their tastes on my lips seemed right.

I rescued four unwrapped loaves of bread from the buzzing flies, plus a bag of uncooked rice. Searching for a passable bottle of red wine, all I got was blank looks.

Wine, senor? *Aqui?*

On the trip back to the Morales compound, I spent time deciphering our directions. I was sitting behind the driver next to Meridyth, who now wore a loose-fitting white top with happy red, purple and yellow embroidery around the neck she had picked up for almost nothing at the market, but I paid little attention.

I did, however, try to time the drive—about 35 minutes from Ojinaga—and decide we were heading almost straight south. Away from the U.S. border, deeper into Mexico. The only road signs I saw promised a place called La Mula. Whatever the hell that was.

In a swirl of dust from the road, we reentered the compound between two large concrete sentinels, looking back as two men wearing machine guns lifted then lowered a thick steel barrier along grooves cut deep into the concrete. A cattle guard, except for men. Going behind the main house to park, I carried the groceries as Meridyth and I were led along a covered breezeway featuring everything but breeze into a smaller structure with dust-clotted exhausts jutting from the roof.

The kitchen was commercial, with two bulky stoves with built-in ovens, each cooktop featuring six gas burners. There was a hood above both ranges, with a fire-retardant system similar to the one at my restaurant. A long stainless-steel prep table off to the side was covered in empty foil trays, bundled plastic wrap and leftover food containers.

"The boss," offered Sanchez, stepping into the kitchen. "Today he is showing his respect, his hospitality. To some of his very important friends." He let out a cynical laugh. "How you say—in high places?"

"I'd figure he'd want my food *for* his party, not after it."

Sanchez gave that missing-tooth laugh. "He doesn't think like you," he said, tapping the side of his head. "That is why he is boss."

After a time, Sanchez trundled Meridyth off to other chores, or perhaps just somewhere to stay beautiful, and left me with only one man pointing a sawed-off shotgun in my direction.

Within five minutes, I was cutting the rabbits into serving pieces, seasoning them with salt and pepper and browning them in batches of off-brand oil—canola, unfortunately, not my preferred extra-virgin olive. The browned pieces went into a large Dutch oven, with all the cut-up vegetables and herbs.

The guard did show me where a couple bottles of cheap red wine were hidden, and I emptied one into the pot. I even tossed in a couple jalapenos I found loose on the shelf. The dish was Provence, by way of Ensenada.

There was something comforting, I have to admit, about the familiar process of it all, the chopping and seasoning and stirring, the forging of order out of chaos. Every night is like that in a busy restaurant, and the order we see emerge is probably the main reason chefs are able to sleep at night.

It was approaching 6 when Sanchez led Meridyth back into the kitchen. She had changed clothes again, this time into a bright yellow sundress.

"Is time," Sanchez said.

"Okay, Commandante, but what's the plan here? I've cooked dinner. Who gets to eat it? When and where?"

"So many questions, senor. We go now to meet Victor Morales. He will explain to you everything."

"Shall I clean up first?"

"Just quickly. The sink." He nodded toward it. "His guests they are leaving. He asks that he to see you. Now."

"Geez." I looked at Sanchez and failed to produce a convincing smile. "He's more trouble than some of my worst best customers."

Drying my hands and face with a towel, I followed Meridyth, who followed Sanchez to a golf cart parked behind the kitchen. This we rode past the helicopters and that ancient plane to what seemed a kind of barn just over a rise from the house.

The first thing I noticed along the outside wall was the long buffet table, buried beneath a turkey carcass and a hotel pan with a few remaining slices of brisket in now-separated barbecue sauce. The second thing was the white-haired man with the gun. Standing out, away from the barn. Away from everything.

Sanchez motioned to us to stay by the table, then stepped out toward the man.

Every ten seconds or so, the stranger with his back to me called out a word I didn't know in Spanish and someone fired a clay pigeon across the sky. With each flight came a swing of the rifle, tracking its arc until the man pulled the trigger and the target exploded. It was like watching shooting stars at night, if the whole point were blasting them out of the sky.

The white-haired man was tall by Mexican standards but appeared smaller because of the stoop in his shoulders and back. From behind, it seemed his legs could barely support his weight. He was thin, almost frail, as though he was slowly disappearing inside his own clothes.

I was watching the man intently when a strange vibration came from the cell phone in my pocket. I knew what the vibration was, though almost no one contacted me this way. And since neither Sanchez nor the man was looking, I quickly checked the phone behind my hand.

The text message was from Jud. And its briefest communication almost stopped my heart.

WE KNOW WHERE U R.

"Senor! Miss Morgan! Come now, please!"

This was Sanchez. I looked up and pocketed my phone. Meridyth moved close to me, took hold of my hand, and we stepped out to meet Victor Morales together.

My mind was reeling. I didn't know what Jud's message meant, or what would happen next. Still, all that stopped—*everything* stopped, if you really want to know—when white-haired Victor Morales turned toward me for the first time, showing me the last face I wanted, needed or expected to see again on this earth. It was an older version of my own.

"Hey Brett," my father said. "How ya been doin', boy?"

"JESUS CHRIST, I THOUGHT you were dead!"

We were sitting by candlelight in my father's Spanish colonial dining room, its heavy, dark-wood table and chairs surrounded by whitewashed plaster walls. He sat at the table's head, sipping better red wine that I'd been able to find in the kitchen—the act alone enough to push me over some barely defined edge. Meridyth and I sat across from each other on either side of him.

My father's bowl was empty after several helpings and several compliments to my improvised rabbit stew, which surely was the first dish of mine ever served by men wearing machine guns. Meridyth the Hollywood vegan had eaten only the vegetables out of hers, and I hadn't touched my food at all.

"Everybody thought you were dead." I was trying to keep my voice even, controlled. I'm not sure how well it worked. "Everybody *told* me you were dead."

"I guess the safest thing to say is: I *was*. Clete Baldwin was dead, wasn't he, Brett? Dead to everybody who mattered. Victor Morales was born a middle-aged drug dealer on the Mexican side of the border. I'm not proud of that, especially not with you coming here now. But he just was."

Sometimes it was an effort to find my father in Morales at all, in this man now wearing a clean guayabera that swallowed him up and a pair of gray pants that seemed tied together at the waist. His long-tanned face had gone pale, with deep wrinkles that drooped from his eyes and around the corners of his mouth. Hastily dampened and pushed straight back from his forehead, his hair was poorly trimmed, covering more and at the same time less than would have been best. And like his shoulders, back and legs, his face was dragged down by a weight that ultimately was beyond him.

"Can I," I asked, looking him in the eye, "even begin to count how many people are *dead* because of you? Will we ever know, really? Did you even bother to keep count."

"No," my father said.

"Well, at least you're honest about *that*. But you know what—I have kept count." I glanced over at Meridyth, and she nodded her sad encouragement. "There's Enrique Morgan and the other 38 guys on top of that mesa. That was pretty cold-blooded, wouldn't you say?"

"Every one of them a criminal. I'm sorry, Meridyth. I hate to say that about your brother, but it's true. By that point, Enrique was just doing what the feds told him to. They were trying to kill me, to take everything I've worked for all these years."

"And while we're talking about Enrique, how about those 19 illegal aliens who died in the back of that truck? His wife was in there. And she was carrying his baby."

"I know that now," my father said. "It was a tragedy. The man who was driving the truck got cold feet, is all. They do that sometimes, no matter how much you pay them. He got a warning about a Border Patrol checkpoint and just parked the truck on the side of the highway. The guy made it back into Mexico within an hour. Of course, he had to be punished."

"You?"

"Not in person, of course. But I made sure it happened. In this culture, putting up with something like that would have been a sign of weakness."

"Is that what it's all about for you? Never showing weakness?"

"Yes, Brett. Sometimes, I'm afraid it is."

"And how about Clay Crawford, that deputy murdered when your thugs took Meridyth from the hospital? And before him, her bodyguard and driver? I mean, *they* weren't criminals—in case that's your excuse for every dead body."

"I know they weren't criminals. But they also weren't killed by me. That was all Johnny Lee Crow. I thought you'd be smart enough to figure that out by now."

"All of them?"

"Yep, every one. At the start, we all figured Enrique had rolled on me. But that wasn't who he gave them. Once Enrique saw how excited the FBI got about a crooked sheriff, that's all he ever told them about. So I went from being afraid of what Enrique had done to being afraid of what Johnny Lee could do. That guy, you know, he would have told them everything. And believe me, after all my years of paying off his Daddy, he knew a helluva lot."

"But he didn't. Tell them anything, I mean."

"No, Johnny Lee didn't tell them anything."

Meridyth looked at me, then at what remained of my father. "May I ask a question?"

He seemed almost surprised. Still, he smiled forgivingly, threaded his fingers together on the table in front of him and nodded his permission for her to speak.

"I really don't understand why you *did* any of this. This wasn't you, it wasn't supposed to be your life. You were a husband, a father. How did all this happen? And why are we even here?

My father cleared his throat, glanced around at each corner of the whitewashed room and rose from his seat.

"Now that's quite a question you've got there, little lady. It sure as hell is."

As Victor Morales, my father stepped to the door, pushed it open a few inches and, in colloquial Spanish that left my translating behind in the dust, ordered the armed guards to leave us alone. They protested, but in the end, Victor Morales was the ultimate boss.

"There." He said to Meridyth and me, standing behind his chair. "That's a little bit better."

He looked at me, holding my eyes.

"Now Brett, I guess I should start by admitting: I was never a very good husband to your mother."

No shit, Sherlock.

Well, that's what I thought. But I decided that interrupting his story one sentence in was neither good manners nor good strategy.

"Some men, I think, weren't put on this earth to be married. And I'm pretty sure I'm one of those men."

"Then why'd the hell you marry my mother?"

"I'm looking at him now," my father said. For me, this was not being the center of attention in any way that was good. "The thing is, Brett, we both thought it would be okay. After you were born, I mean. You have to understand: marriage is *two* people thinking something's going to work, not just one. But it didn't work. I mean, *I* didn't work."

"You had lots of other women. My mother told me that."

"Yes, I did. And I don't have some fancy theory about why that was, but I know now that it hurt her. Hell, I knew it back then. But I couldn't stop." He glanced at me. "Well, I *didn't* stop. It was wrong. I was betraying her, and I was betraying you. But I did it anyway. I did it until the day your mother took you away from me."

"I'm glad you noticed."

"I noticed all right, Brett. It wasn't like I had no feelings. But it was about that time that this thing on the border started. I'll tell you, though. Maybe it did happen, at least a little, because I knew I had nothing left to lose."

"What do you mean?"

"Like I said, there were plenty of women in my life. Most of them for only a night, a few for months or even years. Maria was one of those, a real keeper." He chuckled. "Which means she was nice enough to keep *me,* even though I did her plenty of wrong too."

"Maria? From the café?"

"Sure. The same. It was Maria who set things up so her building went to you when she died. It was her idea all along, not mine. Anyway, it was Maria who got me into this business."

"Smuggling drugs?"

I was so wrong that my father laughed.

"No. In fact, Maria hated drugs. No, smuggling *people.* That came first. And in the beginning, it was only supposed to be one person: her mother. She needed to see a doctor, a specialist, and there wasn't any such thing in her village. Maria asked me to help get her across, and I said I'd try."

"You could have taken her to the river and said, 'Hey, start swimming.'"

"Sure. I could have. But instead, I looked into it, found out everything about it—about the best places to cross, about the people who needed to be paid. Besides, Brett, this lady was real old. It wasn't like we were going to *outrun* anybody. She made it across the river, though, and got to live out her life with Maria in Marfa."

"OK, that's one person," I said. "You could have stopped there, you know."

"Yes, I could have. But by then the word was out. And suddenly every Mexican I met had a mother, brother, sister or cousin he wanted me to bring over."

"Something tells me you didn't do this out of the goodness of your heart."

"Of course I didn't, Brett. I needed to live too. Over time, I got to where I really understood the system. I was already paying off the locals in OJ so they looked the other way, and I'd started making inroads with Johnny Lee's father, who was more than happy to take care of the U.S. side. For a price. You remember, the Border Patrol had its hands full on the Gulf Coast back then. And the Coast Guard was busy with Cubans in inner tubes. So that's how I got into the drug business. And that's how I got *la plaza*.

"The *square?* I don't understand."

"And I," said Meridyth, "don't see how any of that stuff got you into smuggling drugs."

"Around here, *la plaza* is anything. And *la plaza* is everything. It's your ticket, your passport. It's your permit to do business. Somebody always has *la plaza* before you, and you've got to take it from him—usually by killing him. And you have to do all the right things and pay all the right people every month to keep it, while also killing anybody who has his eyes on taking it away from *you*. In this business, people don't go away because you ask them real nice."

"So after a while, it was drugs, not people…?"

"You see, I was already paying off everybody and his brother—literally in many cases—so I could keep taking folks across. But they got greedy, these Mexican officials. They wanted more. Smuggling drugs was never my idea, you gotta understand that. Do you, Brett? Can you? But to get one franchise you had to take the other, see? The drugs were coming in by plane from Colombia by then, landing right outside of town here. If I wanted to move people, I was told, I had to move drugs."

"And that was… fine with you?"

"Brett," my father said, "you probably have no idea the kinds of things a man can talk himself into. Hopefully you'll never have to know, not the way I know it now. You have a million ways to explain every little thing to yourself. And you listen real hard to yourself when it's something you want to hear."

"You figured the drugs were just for the ghettos anyway?" offered Meridyth with sarcasm. "You probably figured they'd get them from somebody. So why not from you?"

"I'm sure that was a part of it. And the thing is, the ghettos *would* have gotten them from somebody anyway. But the strange part is, I was really good at this. It was like I'd built this whole machine, which only got bigger once drugs got involved. Marijuana at first. Then heroin, and finally cocaine. Suddenly I had half the DEA agents in West Texas trying to run me down and the other half trying to shake me down. But when you're a man, Brett—you *have* to understand this—when people depend on you, you do what you need to do."

"You supported Maria this way?"

He laughed. "Hell no, boy. She never took a damn dime from me. All her money, what she had of it anyway, came from that little ole café you ended up with. After a while, she wouldn't even let me buy her flowers or a birthday present, because she knew where the money was coming from. As you might imagine, eventually that was the end of me and Maria. But Brett, she always remembered you. I honestly think she was trying to do the right thing, trying to do a little good with what she left behind in this world."

"So that's it?" I asked. "That's how my honest and honorable father, Clete Baldwin the Texas rancher, became Victor Morales the Mexican drug lord?" I had traveled such a long road in a short time, but I had no earthly idea where I'd ended up. "That's how you became the boss of just about everybody?"

"Brett," he said, his voice as even as I wished mine could be. "I'd have thought your mother would teach you how to listen better than that. The *boss?* Sure, that's what everybody calls you in my position, when they want something from you. How about *this,* boss? Maybe a little more of *that,* boss? But you reach a point when you realize… well, damn it, you're not the boss of *anything.*" His eyes glistened. "And on that day you look all the way up the line at the real bosses, and then finally down the line at all the pathetic pawns. And you know, in a way we're not allowed in this life to know very many things, that you're just another one of *them.* The damn truth is, you're just one more pawn."

Meridyth and I were speechless for a time, both of us gazing at my father from our seats at the table. He didn't say anything either, didn't move. He stood almost without moving, almost without breathing, his hands tightly gripping the back of his chair.

"So," I said finally. "The police and the government are the real drug dealers? But how can that be, really? They're always on TV arresting somebody, or burning a big pile of marijuana."

"That's nothing but public relations, Brett. For one thing, any drugs they destroy are ones that have gone bad, been ruined by water or mildew, whatever. It's just pretty pictures for the cameras."

"And the arrests?"

"Poor sons a' bitches, is all. They either didn't bribe the officials enough, or maybe they were trying to sneak past the controlling families—sneak past *me*—without giving a big enough piece of the action. Around these parts, you know, we really hate freelancers. When the Mexican federales arrest drug smugglers, they're only doing it to protect *us*—the ones who pay them more than their salaries will pay them in a lifetime."

"This thing is upside down. The closer you get to the good guys, the worse they really are?"

"Okay," my father said. "Let me help you out there. This is what happens. Say, you're up for command at the federal police post. You gather enough protection money, enough bribes from the drug smugglers, to pay to get the job—only a downpayment, really. And as part of that deal, you agree how much you'll take from each family each month, what percentage, compared with the guy who had the job before you."

"Okay."

"You also agree with the smugglers what they expect from you for their money—protection for their drugs, obviously, starting the moment they arrive here from Medellin or wherever. But protecting guys like me from competition has become a bigger deal every year. You know, Brett, the governments on both sides of this border tell you this is a "war on drugs." But all it is is a war *for* drugs, and for everybody up the line who's making a buck off of them."

Did I feel sorry for my father? Maybe. But that notion struck me as so outlandish that I struggled against it with everything I had, everything I was. I wouldn't allow myself to feel sorry for him, any more than I'd allow myself to forgive him for anything, for everything he'd done since the day I made my first appearance on this earth.

"So, tell me this, my drug lord." A rock-hard edge found its way into my voice. "What about la guerra?"

"What?"

"The war? You know? I'm told there was a war between two padrinos."

"Shit, boy, that seems like a real long time ago now. That's nothing you need to know about."

"Yes, it is. I want to know about la guerra."

My father reached toward the center of the table, picked up what was left of our wine and motioned toward our glasses. Meridyth and I declined, so he emptied the bottle into his own glass, then drank it off in one long gulp. Reaching up, he brushed his right hand across his lips to wipe off a few purple drops.

"Like I said, that was a real long time ago. Twenty years almost. Back at the beginning. It's always this way, I'm afraid."

"Yes?"

"Brett, do you remember meeting a big fella named Miguel Salazar?" When I didn't respond, my father tried to help me. "He worked around our ranch? I don't know, maybe you were too little to remember. Damn, when you get old, all this shit kinda runs together."

"Miguel Salazar."

"Yeah. At some point, he quit working for me and headed back south, and I figured that was the end of that. But I was wrong. Miguel—I always liked and respected him, I have to tell you that—Miguel came back here, to Chihuahua, and became a real big deal in the drug business. Man, he was in it early, when the hippies just came and shouted across the river to see if anybody had any grass. Somebody always did, you know, and before long Miguel had this whole big network—the same damn hippies mostly—who discovered that bright future in sales the guys in suits in the big cities always talk about. It was like goddamn Amway."

My father looked at me for a laugh, but he didn't get one. He got a quick smile from Meridyth, though, and seemed grateful.

"So years later, when I'm finally forced to start moving drugs along with people, that cut into Salazar's business. Cut bigtime, after a while. But I didn't know. I was still too much of a gringo, I guess. I figured that's just how it was. Competition's a good thing, right? Wrong! The guys I sent north kept getting picked up—Border Patrol, DEA, whoever. Until I finally figured it out. Salazar was tipping them off. Sure, he spread bribes all over the place, just like me. But one of the biggest things he did for the Americans was hand over my shipments, my guys. He practically had a hotline goin' up there."

"And this war broke out."

"Yep. Just a few shootouts at first, with a few guys getting shot in the arm or the leg. But that didn't last very long, and we all ended up wishing we were back in those early days. Gunfights happened all the time, even right in OJ, and nobody was safe. Salazar killed my guys and we killed his, and we both killed whoever got in our way. A whole school bus fulla kids one time, but at least none of the kids died. The driver, though, was killed protecting the kids. Finally the tab included two of Salazar's sons, butchered by two of my people. And I knew my time was up. I had to do something about Salazar—make a deal with him, or kill him—before—"

"Before," I finished my father's sentence, "Salazar could do something about you."

"Yeah." My father looked down at his empty glass. I think he was wishing there was an unlimited supply of wine. He glanced over at Meridyth before his eyes settled on me.

"I went to his ranch—this big old place over by San Carlos, with security to hell and back. Salazar lived very well, of course, better than me back then. I went with just one bodyguard in my battered old Bronco, but I had a whole truckload of my guys armed to the teeth in a truck right behind. I parked in front of Salazar's house and got out of that Bronco alone, an old Army .45 shoved into the back of my pants. I walked up to the front door, seeing no one but knowing we were being watched from all sides. And I knocked on that damn door."

"Welcome wagon?"

"Huh! That's a good one. No, not hardly. Well, Salazar's daughter came to the door, and when I told him who I was there to see, she said he wasn't home. He'd gone into town, she said, or maybe to look at a racehorse somewhere. Whatever it was, it was total bullshit. We'd been watching the house and we knew the old man was home.

"'Now listen here and listen good,' I told this daughter—she musta been in her early 20s—'Your father and I need to talk. I've sent him word that I had nothing to do with the killing of his sons, your brothers. Nothing personal. I am very sad about their deaths, and angry with the men who did these terrible things.' Really, what else could I tell her, Brett? It was true enough, probably. The man and I had to talk, or one of us was going to die. And we were going to take a whole bunch of innocent people with us."

"Did Salazar come out?"

"Nope, the old bastard never did. At one point this daughter, I think her name was Micaela, she got all defiant and said 'To our family, it was *you* who ordered my brothers killed. And it is you who has to pay.' That little gal stared me straight in the face. 'I wish,' she said, 'I could kill you myself right now.'"

"Did she try?" Meridyth asked.

"Well, you really had to be there. I reached behind me with all my guys looking on and slowly pulled out that Army .45. My guys knew to stay cool, I guess, but they knew to be ready too. I pulled out that .45 and handed it right to the daughter. 'If you think it'll end this war,' I said, 'and if you think it'll bring your two brothers back, then you can have what you wish for, right now.' I think she considered it. But she also considered the fact that as quick as she could kill me, my men would tear her up. And then there were probably men ready to tear them up. Without saying a thing, she pressed the gun back toward me. And disappeared inside."

"So the war went on?" asked Meridyth

"Yes, it did. For another 15 minutes."

"What are you saying?" This was me.

"Salazar, more crazy than stupid by this point—crazy with grief over his sons—had set up an ambush on our way out toward the gates of his ranch, where his land joined the old highway to Camargo. There was this dip in the caliche road, this gully, probably on old dried-up river bed. And when both our vehicles had gone down in there, with all this dust swirling to blind us, a whole bunch of Salazar's guys opened up on us with everything they had. Uzis, Kalashnikovs—man, it was like the Battle of the Bulge."

"I'm surprised you're still around."

"You and me both. But we did our best defending ourselves, jumping out, using our trucks for cover, shooting wherever the shots were coming from. And I guess we were lucky. After what seemed like a lifetime, maybe 4 or 5 minutes, the firing died down and the smoke and dust could start to settle. There were all of our guys, many of them dead or dying, and most of Salazar's guys just dead. So when we're checking the bodies, who turns up but Salazar himself, still alive, barely. My guys shouted out when they found him, and I walked over. I was covered in grime and bleeding from my forehead, but I could tell the stubborn old man recognized me by the look on his face. I looked at him for a long time, you know, watching the life flood out of him right along with all his blood. Finally I bent over close to his face. 'I'm real sorry,' I said, 'about your sons.' And I blew his brains out."

The silence in the dining room seemed to spread from our table, smothering the sounds of everything on earth.

"I'm not sure I was myself then," my father said. "Or hell, maybe that's *exactly* who I was. I got a rope from my Bronco and tied Miguel Salazar a few feet behind, and I dragged his body over the rocks and cactus all the way back to his house. Blowing the horn long and hard, I made two then three circles of the house, aware that every window was full of people looking out. I heard screams and wailing from inside, but I kept going round and round, even though I didn't know why. Finally I stopped, cut the body free and glared at that house with more hatred than I'd ever felt before or since. They could have killed me right then, I knew. But nobody did a damn thing. The daughter came out finally, weak and shaking, crying hopelessly. Just stood there looking at me. And I looked at her. And anything I ever had inside of me that was human, well, it broke off like its own iceberg and drifted away. I climbed back into my Bronco and drove out through the front gate. And Brett, that war you asked me to tell you about? It ended on that day."

I said nothing. I wasn't 100% sure I'd ever feel up to speaking again.

"So." Meridyth broke the silence, after an eternity. "I'm sorry, but I think you forgot to answer one of my questions."

"Which question was that?"

"Mr. Morales, you haven't told us what *we* are doing here."

"Oh honey." My father smiled through his exhaustion. "I'd have gotten around to that sooner or later."

"How about now?" This time it was me. "You should give some serious thought to answering now."

"Hell, boy, that damn question has been on my mind a long time. I don't have to give it any thought at all. Why do you think I sent our guards away?"

"I have no idea."

Clete Baldwin looked affectionately at Meridyth and then moved his gaze over to me, and for the briefest of moments a whole lot of awful things didn't exist or seem to matter anymore.

"Because," he said, "it's time I turned myself in. And I need you to help me do it."

I WOKE WITH A START, alone in the narrow bed.

Not that I expected to be with anyone—*wanting* is something else again—or in a different bed, since I remembered I was in a drug lord's compound 20 miles south of the U.S. border. No, it was something else that woke me, a thought shooting across my brain in the middle of a dream. And then I remembered.

I reached over the side of the bed and lifted my boots off the scuffed plank floor. Switching on the bedside lamp, I shook each one out onto the bed; that produced only a small pile of dust, which I brushed off where I'd be sure to step in it later. I ran my fingers along all the places where leather met leather, with stitching to hold things together.

Then I carefully, inch by inch, went over the bottom of the soles. After coming up empty on the first boot, I found what I suddenly suspected on the second.

There was a tiny—I mean, tiny enough no one would notice and, until now, none of the bad people checking me had noticed—almost microscopic slit in the bottom of my left boot. It's the kind of slit or rip that sometimes picks up a pebble and drives you insane till you work or shake it out. This time the slit had picked up a digital transmitter, a device smaller than any pebble I'd ever seen.

I smiled. The FBI hadn't done this. All the surveillance equipment they'd hung on me in Marfa hadn't done this. My work was done, they'd said. But Jud had known better. There were too many people out to hurt me this time, and too many places they could take me to do it.

"Goddamn it, Jud!" I said too loudly. The door to the room swung open and a guard with a machine gun inquired, "Senor?" I nodded that all was well and, wanting all to be well, he pulled the door back shut.

Moments later, the door opened again, just enough that I could see the guard's leer, an expression no one on earth does better than a Mexican living along the U.S. border. There must be a special school for it. Then he pushed the door a bit farther, enough to reveal Meridyth standing there in a robe that reached her ankles. He motioned her into the room with his machine gun and then, with another leer in my direction, pulled the door shut.

"I couldn't sleep," she said, arms crossed in front of her, her gaze wandering to the floor and around to the walls before settling reluctantly on me. "So when I heard you moving, I thought, well, maybe he'd let me come visit for a while."

"Of course you can." I nodded toward the door. "But how'd you talk our new best friend into letting you?"

"There is little on this earth that a bribe can't accomplish." She giggled. "Turns out, this place isn't all that different from Hollywood."

"Pesos?"

"Actually, dollars work fine. I'm glad I had some on me."

"So now we know."

I smiled and pressed my body toward the wall, drawing the sheet up around me to form a clean, flat surface. I patted the spot lightly. Drawing her robe tight around her, Meridyth slid gently onto it.

"You know, Brett, I think we're spending entirely too much time sitting at each other's bedsides."

"Afraid what the tabloids would say, you mean?"

"No, I'm just thinking we can do better than bed*sides*."

"And, well, as for you not being able to sleep," I said, trying to master the official Mexican leer, "another time and another place, I might be able to help you out with that."

"It's so good to know you've grown up since high school."

"Absolutely."

Meridyth turned to me, her eyes not laughing anymore.

"Brett, are you okay with this? Your father being alive, I mean?"

"Nobody ever asked me," I said, "if I was okay with anything before."

"*I'm* asking."

The best I could do was, "I don't know." Deciding that wasn't much of a verbal legacy, I pushed ahead. "It's weird, is all. But everything feels different now. I don't know why it does, but everything is different with him alive."

Never in my life had there been less doubt about who "him" was.

"I have…" I said, and when I stopped for lack of words she softly covered my hand with hers. "I have these thoughts. About things that happened. Or things that never happened. And how they all would have been so different. You know?"

"Yes, I do."

"And I think about my mother, all the stuff he put her through. And that always makes me hate him. But then I meet him, here, a different person than he ever was. Certainly a different person than I *thought* he was. And… and, the thing is, I don't know if I can hate him so much anymore."

"And that," she said, a statement more than a question, "makes the world a different place."

I looked up from the sheets, where I had riveted my gaze for the longest time. Meridyth was looking down at me, her eyes deep pools of warm liquid, the simplest hint of a smile forming on her lips.

"Yes," I said. "It does."

She reached over and switched off the lamp. As the room sifted into blue darkness, I felt Meridyth rise from her preordained spot and then heard her robe fall into a pile on the floor.

"Brett," she said, "I'd really like you to hold me now."

Without thinking, I lifted the edge of the sheet that covered me and felt her slip in alongside. She was wearing a thin nightgown, just something to sleep in. But Meridyth was underneath the fabric, and that was all that mattered.

"Nice," I said.

She laughed. "Been a while for you, has it, sailor?"

"Oh yes."

"Me too. Believe it or not."

"I'm shocked."

"I guess," Meridyth said, and then she laughed nervously. In the darkness, I felt her turn her face from me, as though she were too shy to let me see her speaking, which I of course couldn't anyway. "Oh God, Brett, you're gonna think I'm nuts. I mean, it's not like I go around telling any of this to people."

"Telling them what?"

"About you, silly."

"Why would you tell anybody about me? Even more, what would you tell them? I mean, all we did was see each other at some football game. And after that, all I did was make a damn fool of myself at a dance. Come on, that was a lifetime ago, Meridyth. We've both done so much in between."

"I know we have, Brett. It's just…"

"Just what?" I felt my face flush with embarrassment. "I mean, I'm surprised you even remember any of it. You were the prettiest girl in the whole school, trying to enjoy a holiday dance with her boyfriend."

"Yes, Matt was my boyfriend," Meridyth said. "Until that night."

"What's that mean?"

"After that night, after I asked you to meet me at the water tower, Matt *wasn't* my boyfriend anymore."

"Oh Meridyth, why the hell are you dragging me back to high school? Wasn't it horrible enough the first time?"

I felt her body stiffen, as though every inch of her flesh and blood had reached some difficult decision, had arrived at a long-feared place with no way out. Except pushing straight ahead.

"Brett, I went, you know."

"Went?"

"To the water tower, I mean. That Friday night. Like I said in the note."

"You did?"

"Of course I did. And it was damn cold out there too. Like freezing. But you, sir, never showed up."

"No, I didn't."

"And I broke up with Matt right before I went to meet you. I called him on the phone and told him I didn't want to go out with him anymore. And I did that, you see, because I knew what I wanted. Sure, I was only 14. But I knew from that moment in that gym that I wanted to be with you."

"But—but—"

"Nicely put."

"But—you didn't call *me* on the phone. You really might have, you know. I would have answered. We could have talked. And I would have loved every word."

"I know that now. Don't you think I've thought of it, this whole time? That I've beaten up on myself through a movie career, several entirely stupid affairs with married men, and one horrific marriage? All because of that *one* damn phone call I didn't make, when I was 14? I wanted, you see, to tell you I loved you in person. I wanted to hold your hand like in the movies and look into your eyes and tell you everything I felt and hoped and wanted in the whole world."

"At 14?"

"Okay," she giggled, "so I was mature for my age."

"Apparently." I kept struggling to put the pieces together, but in my head they all kept falling apart again. "Meridyth, you never—Why didn't you tell me when we came back from—" I stopped suddenly as the memory of that time tackled me, the memory I'd kept buried, and made it impossible for me to go on. "Oh my God. I understand."

"It's about time."

"I never *did* come back, did I?"

"You moved to Houston."

"Yes, I did."

"And you'll never know what it was like for me that first day after Christmas break. Asking everybody where you were, of course without wanting to sound like I was asking everybody where you were. No one knew, Brett. *No one.* I finally had to go to the school office. And all the ladies there could tell me was that you were no longer registered. I thought—no, I *knew*—my life was over. And in some strange and terrible way that nobody with a brain would ever believe, it really *was* over, Brett. From that day in that high school office. Until tonight."

I felt her turn her face back to me in the darkness, the past no longer a thing one person had to suffer through alone, suddenly a place two people could grow from together. The past had arrived, had emerged from the shadows of its dark labyrinth, to share this bed with us. But for the first time in either of our lives, it was something we did not fear.

Meridyth snuggled into my arms, and I felt her pressing against my bare chest, her warm soft breath brushing my cheek.

"Brett, the thing is, honey—besides our rather serious lack of privacy here, I don't want this to be our first time. I want something special for us, something we've deserved for a long time, something we'll always remember."

"I'm pretty sure I'll remember this—"

"You have a point. But you know? Maybe with champagne. Or at least a nightgown I'd actually want you to see me in."

"Nightgowns," I pointed out, kissing her cheek. "Highly overrated."

We found each other's lips then. It was like the first kiss except it wasn't and it had no end, starting then stopping then starting again, each time a little different and a lot more intense, a long tunnel of doors swinging open to take us deeper and deeper inside. Arms and legs became an entangled mess beneath the sheet, as did her nightgown and the boxers I sometimes couldn't tell if I still had on. And then, with a final kiss as punctuation, Meridyth pulled away with one soft and delicious groan.

"Soon, lover," was all she said. *"Soon."*

She turned and at first I feared she was leaving me, wondering how desperate, how violent I might get to keep her here in my bed. But she was simply turning in place, backing into the arch my body formed and pulling my arms tight around her.

"This is my favorite," she said.

"Hmm, it's kind of growing on me too."

Meridyth laughed.

The night was silent outside our window. And whatever our guard had heard through the door or thought behind his leer, he was silent as well. There was only us in the darkness, and I caught myself thinking I'd waited my entire life for a moment exactly like this.

"Hey," said Meridyth, "you feel very good back there."

"I'm kinda hard to miss right now."

"Yes," she said, "if you insist on being so literal about it."

Meridyth and I kept telling each other we were too excited to sleep. We slept until the sun was shining.

"YOU CAN'T BE A DRUG DEALER, I guess," said Morales, "if you don't have a whole bunch of cell phones."

As planned the night before, the three of us stood in the bright sunshine at the edge of the compound's vast holdings, the dusty old drug plane and the quartet of helicopters a distant memory now.

During the night, three large boxy trucks had taken up residence in front of the house—we saw them as soon as we stepped outside. They were the sort of vehicles that probably worked for U-Haul 350,000 miles ago. By this point, "last legs" were two of the kinder words you could use to describe them. The cargo gate at the back of each truck was rolled up, a warehouse awaiting its cargo. And there, in a makeshift pen of chicken wire, was some of the saddest-looking cargo I had ever seen.

Dressed in rags, or what used to be rags when they were nicer, dark-skinned men, women and children sat, lay, stood, squatted and slumped, sometimes seemingly a mix of all those things. There was no joy in their eyes, no excitement about a new life waiting with the next dawn—just exhaustion and what I took to be fear. Even without newspapers, radio or television, they'd heard the same horror stories we all have.

Now perhaps three miles away from that scene, Meridyth and I looked on as Morales dug through a leather satchel before offering me a small rectangle of technology.

"And I have his number," I said, dredging a crumpled business card from my pocket.

Morales was nodding at me, ready for me to make the call, when the walkie talkie riding his belt erupted in a frenzy of angry Spanish. Morales rolled his eyes and whispered the word "Sanchez" before responding.

"Si, Commandante."

It was hard for me to keep up, but Sanchez was berating my father—more angrily than I would have expected, really—for leaving the house without bodyguards. He said he would send a team immediately. In fact, he threatened to do this several times, each time to hear my father overrule him.

"No," said Victor Morales. "There will be no guard as I interrogate the prisoners. We must make our demands public today, and I alone must determine what those demands will be."

"But it's too dangerous." Even over the distortion-filled walkie talkie, it was clear that danger was not the real issue. It was something else, but crossing languages and crossing sides, I couldn't begin to guess what.

"Sanchez, let me ask you something, because maybe you forgot."

"Yes? What?"

"Who has *la plaza* here? You or me?"

There was silence, and again the feeling that there was some larger story being told hung over all the moments that passed without an answer.

"You do, senor."

"Then, I will return as soon as I am finished here."

"Si, claro. Senor."

Victor Morales turned to Meridyth and me, shaking his head. "I'm thinking we picked a fine time to be doing this."

The call on the cell phone went straight through.

"Mills," he answered, a whole country but less than 100 miles away.

I filled the FBI agent in on my whereabouts, told him I was with Meridyth Morgan as prisoners of Victor Morales. I described the compound quickly, in terms of how many men—perhaps 40 I'd caught glimpses of, with surely more waiting in OJ. I described the road out from town as best I could.

"So, Morales… Is he looking to trade? Ransom? What? We're gonna do our best to get you and Meridyth back here."

"That may be easier than you think."

"What do you mean?"

"Victor Morales wants to turn himself in. To the FBI, though, not to anybody here—for obvious reasons." The picture of Johnny Lee Crow's lifeless body popped up, but I pressed it back down. "And listen, Mills. Morales wants *me* to bring him in."

"Do you think he's telling the truth?"

I glanced at my father. "Yes, I do."

"God, Brett." The agent finally let himself sound happy. "That's terrific. I can speak to *him* about this?"

"Sure. He figured you'd want to."

I nodded to my father, who took the phone from my hand.

"Agent Mills, my… well, this fellow Brett here has told me you're a straight shooter. So I'm gonna treat you like one. And, don't worry. I was born in the U.S., or at least in Texas." Morales smiled at his little joke. "So don't worry about me not sounding Mexican enough, okay? I can sound it when I need to."

Mills said something.

"Sure, we can talk about that," said Morales. "The local federales, sure, and the ones in the capital they paid off to get here. You won't have any problem believing me. Once we talk."

More Mills, and what little I might have picked up was drowned out by the stinging wind.

"Yep, that's fine. I can give 'em all to you, if you want. Or you can just turn a couple and use 'em, if that's better. You probably know a lot of this, right? The thing is: you can know 'em all you want, but if you don't have anybody to testify against 'em in court, you got nothin'."

From the look on my father's face, Mills agreed.

"Okay," he said. "You work on that. But look, two things, Mills. It's got to be tonight. Big shipment heading your way, after midnight. Just west of Lajitas, where the river's a mud puddle. Three trucks, crossing together but then splitting up. One up to Alpine, one up to Marfa, and the other all the way to Odessa. Illegals and cocaine. Enough of both to make some serious charges stick."

"We like it when that happens," I heard the agent say.

"Be best if you can take all three trucks at once. We'll be armed, so you better make it one hell of a surprise. I'll be driving the truck with the white cab, and my two hostages will be with me. I'd appreciate it if you'd arrest me then. And kill me when I try to escape."

"You're not thinking about trying to escape, are you, Mr. Morales?"

"Not on your life."

I could almost hear Mills working through the action steps. "And the second thing?" he asked.

"You can forget 'hands across the border' and all that shit. I'd suggest you don't tell anybody over here what you're planning to do."

Mills asked to talk to me again.

"Brett, I think we can do this."

"How long?"

"Few hours, I hope. Cut me some slack here. We'll get the DEA involved, the Border Patrol and U.S. Customs. And while I think we can make the terrorism rationale stick—to my way of thinking, it sticks already—it's always a hell of a lot easier to sell when it's Pakistan. People don't get the right picture when the terrorists are wearing sombreros."

"Mills, I haven't seen a damn sombrero yet. A lot of machine guns, though, and a few Bushmasters and a sawed-off shotgun or two."

"Gosh," Mills said, "I didn't know you cared."

"I just want you to know."

"Copy that," Mills said.

"And one more thing. Is Jud with you? I called his cell this morning. He sent me a text saying he knew where we were, but now I can't reach him. So if he's with you, tell him what's going on, okay?"

At the far end of the signal, Mills didn't breathe for several long seconds.

"Well, that's just it," he said. "Harris and I have been leaving messages for him too. I'm thinking he's already down there. In Mexico somewhere."

The three of us climbed back into the Jeep—the old-fashioned, open military kind, not the Cherokee that became the Liberty—and headed back over the deeply rutted track to the house. With Morales driving, raising a thick plume of dust behind us, we climbed over the final rise and looked down on the house.

Morales stopped the Jeep atop the rise, then scanned the scene with binoculars from under the driver's seat. Silently, he set them down and began a slow trip down, looking worried.

I remember noticing the position of the buildings for the first time, scattered around the bottom of a bowl inside their perimeter of concrete and steel. I felt Morales slow the Jeep as the three of us realized together there were no guards at the main house, no trucks, and no immigrants outside in the chicken-wire pen.

Morales kept the Jeep moving, in through the gate, past the plane, the helicopters and several Jeeps like our own. The compound was silent— dead, really, as though all the armed men he paid to work for him had been wiped off the board by an unseen hand.

The FBI? No, too soon for them.

Jud?

"You wait here," Morales said severely, halting the vehicle in front of the house, hopping out onto the dirt. "Let me see what this is all about."

Meridyth and I glanced at each other and, in a moment of wordless conspiracy, jumped out too, following steps behind as he walked up to the front door. He was almost there when it opened and a pistol emerged, followed by a dark hand on the grip, followed by Commandante Pablo Sanchez.

"Welcome, Senor Morales," Sanchez said, grinning from beneath his mustache. He moved forward, eyes blazing, until the pistol almost touched my father's forehead. "You did not take my warning seriously enough, I think."

"Sanchez, what the hell are you doing?" My father's voice gained force, as though he would call down the wrath of God at any moment. "*What* is the meaning of this?"

"Meaning, senor?" As Sanchez spoke, three more gunmen came out through the door, training their guns on Morales. Another ten came around the sides of the house, several opting to cover Meridyth and me. "You have been in this business a long time, senor. I would think you would give up on *meaning*."

Sanchez pressed Morales a couple steps backward with his pistol, grinning wildly. At the last instant, he tilted the gun and fired high into the air. The sound echoed off all the rises, and it dawned on me, from the way the men's eyes darted about, that it had been a signal.

"Look, my old friend," said Sanchez, nodding. "*That* will have to be your meaning."

Morales backed away from the gun enough to turn his head, and as our eyes followed, we saw black vehicle after black vehicle come up over the nearest rise and disgorge soldiers in full battle armor, their helmets and visors glinting in the sun. Carrying riot shields and what appeared to be rocket launchers, the troops made their way down in front of the house, dark personnel carriers edging up close to form a noose around us.

I was standing behind my father, but I'm pretty sure he laughed in Sanchez's face, even though he made no sound.

"The federal *police?*" he asked. "That's really good, you know. That's perfect. Just like they did with Camarena, who I saved you from? And oh, just like with Acosta before that?"

"Yes," said Sanchez. "It is their job, isn't it, these troops—to hunt down the drug lords. To arrest them. To *kill* them. It is a shame you tried to fight back." The commandante grinned. "It is a shame you and your hostages were all killed in the gunfight."

"So," my father said. "This is your doing."

"I would ask you, senor," Sanchez said in better English than I knew him to possess. "Who has *la plaza* now?"

FOR THE NEXT FOUR HOURS, the three of us sat in the room—my room, the one with the seriously rumpled bedclothes—waiting to be killed. We spoke to each other occasionally, but were silent for long stretches.

"What the hell are they *doing?*" my father exploded finally, sitting in a straight-back chair, his head twisting in his hands. Meridyth and I sat on the edge of the bed, our bodies careful not to touch. "I can't figure out what's going on out there."

"Waiting for orders to kill us?"

"Maybe," he said. "But not likely. *I* never waited."

We'd seen many a conference beyond our window, some involving Sanchez and some not. A few had turned nasty, with either the Commandante or an officer of the federal police making loud phone calls. Our two guards, who never left the room, seemed amused by the whole big show—but never enough to set down their Bushmasters.

"Look at it this way," I said to my father. "Being alive is always better than being dead."

I caught the edge of a smile.

"I guess that's why men have sons: to supply them with pearls of wisdom like that."

"I suppose so. Yes."

About half an hour later, the guards were arguing—about *futbol*, I think—when a single vibration rippled through the phone in my pocket. As before, with my eyes glued to the guards, I moved the phone out of my pocket, flipped it open and found the latest missive from Jud. His text messages were getting shorter all the time.

D DAY

The gunfire began small and far away, picking off platoons of federales on the outskirts of the property. But rolling like a wave heading in to shore, the noise and confusion moved closer, a burst of fire here, an explosion there. By now, the guards had forgotten about *futbol*. They aimed their Bushmasters at the closed door and waited for someone to try to take us from them.

There were shouts from outside our window, men trying to organize themselves, and then other shouts that sounded more like screams.

My father, Meridyth and I did our best to huddle as bullets raked across the side of the house. Through the space between the curtains, we saw huge fireballs shoot into the air as one after another of the helicopters exploded, their remaining fuel sending up coiling serpents of thick black smoke.

Eyes wide with terror, the guards turned their guns on us.

A tangle of sounds erupted at that moment right outside the window, an explosion spitting fire and rounds fired off in all directions by an army. Instinctively, the guards spun toward the noise and opened fire, ripping a hole twice as big as what had been there before.

They kept on firing, even as we all started to process the sounds, to redefine them not as someone attacking but as explosive charges set all around us. For the two screaming guards, that realization came a second too late.

The door kicked open and, as they turned, Jud Garcia stepped into the room and used his Smith & Wesson to drill one guard through the center of the forehead and his Glock to blow the other's jaw away. Their bodies hadn't settled on the floor before Jud kicked them out of our way.

"Hey, I brought your favorite," he said, thrusting the Remington into my hands.

Jud recognized my father where Victor Morales should have been and made a quick calculation of friend or foe, which at the moment was more than my father's only son could do. "Hmm," was his only comment, followed by, "Let's go."

Trailing Jud, the three of us moved into the smoke-filled hall, turning left toward the front door. Jud stopped, listened to the cracking and snapping of a fire his explosions had set off and the screams of the federal police and the rounds fired by the troops he'd brought with him.

"Change of plans," he said, pressing back past us in the hall to lead us the opposite way, toward another door we'd noticed but never tried to use.

"Jud," I said, as we moved, one foot at a time. "Who's out there with you?"

"Oh them guys?" he said, grinning at me through the smoke. "Just a few Injuns who like to get off the reservation."

"Injuns?"

"Well, okay. That's a metaphor. I think."

"Jud." I studied the spaces on his face between the grit. "Is that war paint you're wearing?"

"Sure," he said over his shoulder. "Didn't you read the invitation?"

The back door was locked from outside, but the Bushmaster made quick work of that. Jud shoved the door with his foot, aimed the weapon outward and rolled into the sunshine in front of him, spraying two policemen in the same motion.

Jud nodded toward the barn and, with him hanging back to cover us, we sprinted to it and into it, deep slices of dust-filled sunlight falling hard across dry, ancient hay. The sounds of battle, however, shifted in our direction, with bullets pinging through the rotted walls. We had to move on.

Again, Jud provided cover. I could see him firing the Bushmaster around the corner, the S&W in his shoulder holster, the Glock in the back of his belt, and the slight bulge of the Airweight at his ankle. It was a good look for Jud.

"Follow me," he said, eyes focused on the open ground we had to cross.

Jud pushed away from the barn and sprinted across a 30-yard stretch, rolling once as a flurry of bullets found him but back on his feet to return the fire. He made it to a large chunk of helicopter, a tangle of torn metal with smoke pouring from one end, then looked back to summon us. With a roar from deep in his chest, he rose up to full height and set about slaughtering everything that dared cross his path.

I grabbed Meridyth and my father, and we ran.

Landing hard beside Jud, sheltered now behind the copter carcass, we each must have wondered why we'd invested so much in making it here just to die. But Jud nodded over his shoulder between angry bursts of his Bushmaster, and we finally understood.

The old plane was close, waiting like a jetliner at some poor man's LaGuardia.

"Can you," he asked my father, "fly that damn thing?"

"It's been a while. But sure."

"Good," Jud said.

Sensing a lull in the battle, Jud rose up and, sweeping his gun across the horizon, backed to the side of the plane nearest the door. He reached up his free hand and yanked twice before the door came down, showering him with dust that stuck to his sweat as rickety, rope-tied steps discovered contact with the ground.

Just as Jud made it back behind the copter, a platoon of federal police rushed from the barn, hunting us; but Jud proceeded to return the favor one dead federale at a time. He shoved us out with one hand and we ran for the steps, my father starting up first.

And that's how we were—my father midstep halfway, Meridyth approaching the bottom, and me out in the open—when Commandante Sanchez stepped from behind the plane's tail.

"Morales!"

I saw it all: my father frozen in shock, Meridyth's mouth opening into a scream, the terrible scar on Sanchez's face. The machine gun in his hand kept rising, sucking the air out of my lungs with every inch of its arc. But it wasn't rising alone.

The thunderous explosion caught Sanchez from the side, filling his military shirt with red dots that merged into one as flame devours a thin sheet of paper. He was lifted off his feet and then, with a surprised look quickly going blank, planted in the dust beside the plane. It appeared that not a single pellet from my Remington had been wasted.

The cranking of the diesel brought me back, a choking sound from within the plane, then scratching, dragging and tearing as the propellers struggled to turn. They *did* turn, first one and then the other. My father was inside the cockpit, Meridyth waving me aboard.

I started up the steps and suddenly, as something grabbed my attention, ran back down and kicked the wooden blocks from the tread-bare rubber tires. At the top of the steps, I turned and waved to Jud, still fighting his ground war, then snagged the rope that held them together and yanked the doorway shut behind me.

"That's better," my father said, moving the plane forward as though it were yelling back at him. One foot, then another, then feet in twos, fours and eights as he straightened the nose across a wide stretch that had the benefit of no particular war going on.

He caught me looking around the cabin, its floor littered with hay, chicken feathers and what probably were several controlled dangerous substances, for someplace Meridyth and I could be safe.

"Y'awl better hold on," he said calmly. The plane picked up speed even as it picked up attention, the first bullets tearing in one side and pinging out the other. "We have to climb fast, or else they'll shoot us down."

There were worn leather straps on each side of the cockpit. Meridyth grabbed one, I the other. We felt the plane edge off the ground, settle back with a grinding thud, then lift off and stay that way.

My father pulled back on the stick hard, and I saw his face grimacing as our speed increased along with our trajectory. We were almost lifted off our feet, only the straps keeping us anchored. It was like riding a subway shot from a cannon.

Minutes passed, the sounds of Jud's dark battle falling farther beneath us. After a lot of protesting, the twin propellers settled into a mostly smooth drone.

"Brett!"

This was Meridyth, squeezing my arm as we leveled out enough that we could stand. She was pointing out through the cockpit window, and all of us saw the long green line of the river snaking its way through the purple mountains of Big Bend National Park.

"The border," my father smiled. "I don't know about you two, but that's where I want to be headed right about now."

And then, right about now was when it happened.

The plane shook violently, as though something huge grabbed it and waved it about. Meridyth and I were thrown to the floor, cutting ourselves on piles of wire and broken crates. When we recovered, my father was still at the controls, but a Niagara of blood was pouring from the top of his head.

"Goddamn missile," he growled. "Look at that shit, will you?"

We followed his gaze out the window to where the propeller on the right side—indeed most of the right wing—popped and sizzled in flame and smoke that turned the dust-covered gray to black. Each time the engine stuttered, a balloon of thick, dark smoke escaped behind us into the air.

My father wiped the red fountain from his eyes with his sleeve, then reached under his seat and the empty seat next to him. He tossed two satchels in our direction.

"Put those on! Now!" he said. "You're gonna need 'em!"

"What about you?"

He seemed about to chuckle, but a stream of blood choked him off.

"Damn plane only comes with two," he said, then struggled to laugh again. "I shudda bought the deluxe package."

As Meridyth and I wiggled into our parachutes, we caught glimpses of the world flashing and spinning outside the window. The view was wild and dislocated, as the engine belched fire and smoke on its way to stopping altogether.

I couldn't see the river anymore, but then, obliging me in a heart-stopping way I wouldn't want to repeat, the plane lurched down and forward and I could see we were directly above it. There were green trees and tall green grass alongside the river a thousand feet below and, even at the deadly height of West Texas summer, stretches of blue-green water shimmered deep in its bed.

Meridyth smiled, but she was cut short by my father.

"Open that door," he shouted above the roar, a thousand small explosions growing closer to becoming one. "Kick it open if you have to."

I turned the rusted latch but, as predicted, the door wouldn't budge. I kicked it once, feeling like my knee was coming back through my chin, but the damn thing was solid, as though somebody had welded us inside.

"Again!" my father shouted.

I did, and then again. And then without warning the door didn't just open but tore off whatever passed for hinges and plummeted with twisting agony to the desert floor. If Meridyth hadn't grabbed me by the belt and held on, I would have gone out with it.

The roar of the wind was deafening now, the cabin a drunk's worst nightmare of things crashing and slicing and shredding through the air. I felt the plane rising, my father pulling back on the stick. The blood was horrific, soaking through the top of his shirt and spilling onto the equipment all around him.

"Now," he said, turning to face us, looking me straight and hard in the eyes. "Get your asses off this plane!"

We did, me pushing Meridyth out the door before she could think about it and then following right behind her—before *I* could think about it. By some miracle, those two parachutes were the only thing on that plane that worked. And the gift of altitude my father had given us let them fly open above us till they grabbed the air with a painful but oh-so-welcome tug.

Meridyth and I watched speechless as my father's plane lost one engine and then the other, the universe taking on a silence as horrifying as death. Losing speed and lift, the plane tipped its wings back and forth in ancient salute, then plowed a deep furrow into the mountainside before exploding in a rising, widening ball of flame.

JUD FOUND US AS THE SUN started down, grinding his F-350 into the clearing where we huddled in our parachutes like Ishmael pulled from a cruel sea.

He tried to talk us into going home but, in the end, simply followed as Meridyth and I made our way on foot deeper into Big Bend, climbing to track our visual memory of everything we'd seen as we floated back to earth.

"The boot, Jud," I said finally, trying not to run out of air as we struggled upward. "The transmitter, I mean. That was good."

"Yeah," he said, not winded at all. "It was."

The colors that usher in night enveloped our procession as it topped the final rise, and all around us the stillness was sifting in ambers, purples and blues. To the west glowed a bright rim where the sun had just been, and then even that was gone.

Small fires lit our way along the furrow dug by the plane. At times we had to cover our faces through smoke. Other times, the air was fresh, with an edge of night's chill pressing in.

"There," Meridyth said.

A cliff rose above us at the end of the furrow, and there the wreckage smoldered. The plane had run hard against the wall, its nose broken off and pointing to the side. The wings too had severed, finding resting places in odd pieces and strange angles along the fiery path. One tall, thin piece of wing had lodged in the dirt, rising above the final pile like a flag.

"Over here," my father said weakly.

Clete Baldwin lay to the side of the wreckage, perhaps having been thrown there, perhaps having crawled there to escape the flames. From the look of his body, that was as far as he ever would crawl.

"The compound," he murmured, disoriented. "Jud? The FBI?"

"Showed up eventually, once they got the Mexican government to invite them." Jud smiled. "I never have been much for asking permission myself. Something tells me this is a story you'll never see on CNN."

"CNN?" my father asked.

"From the way they were picking up bodies, I think *both* governments want this one to go away."

"Jud, it was good—of you—to come for us."

"Some things in this life, you're supposed to do yourself."

"I know," my father said.

I stepped forward, and he looked up at me, grimacing through the sheets of caked blood on his face.

"This hurts like a son of a bitch, you know."

"I'm sorry. We'll get help. You'll…"

"Stop it, Brett, okay? You ain't doing any such thing." Was that the slightest smile crossing his dried-out lips? "I've done my deal. Now you need to go and do yours. It's that simple, really."

"How come it doesn't *feel* simple?"

"Because, boy, it never does."

He nodded to Meridyth standing beside me, then turned his eyes to Jud. There was quiet pleading in them, and at first I didn't understand. Jud nodded with finality, a promise to keep, and my father seemed to find peace.

"I wanted—" He couldn't go on at first, but he cleared his throat, shook his head till his eyes reopened. "I wanted to do more—I mean, be more—I was always so hard—on you—and your mother."

I knelt beside him and set my hand lightly on his shoulder. He knew my hand was there, even though he couldn't turn his head to see it.

"I know," I said, wondering how so few words could mean so much. "It's okay, Dad. Really."

I stood up slowly then, daring to glance at Jud, then feeling Meridyth thread her arm through mine.

"Come on, Brett," she said, almost in a whisper. "Let's go home."

Backing away, I picked out one small detail in the firelight. The bottom of Jud's jeans had snagged on the ankle holster that held his Centennial Airweight. The holster was empty.

Meridyth and I turned and started down the trail, passing from firelight into deepening darkness. We stopped when we heard the shot but didn't look back. I knew Jud was saying his prayers for the spirit that would hover above our heads forever. I knew he was sprinkling holy water on the blood of Big Clete Baldwin. My animal. My ancestor.

I took my first step forward. And all the ones after that.